AF244188

Edited by DR. Indigo and Liz Taylor. Thank you so much for your input and enthusiasm.

ISBN 978-0-9921543-0-1

Corner of Your Eye Publishing

Ontario, Canada. N2Z 2X3

fromthecornerofyoureye@gmail.com

What goes around,

FEEDS THE GROUND

book one

the Farm

INTRODUCTION

My friends, this is a story that is still unfolding, no matter today's date. An acquaintance of a friend, of a friend of mine plays a small role through legend in this early stage of the tale. He will have a much greater impact on our main character in the decades, and centuries to come, but, of course, that is another story in itself.

Our leading man, Collin, who was left to die as a baby, neglected and beaten as an orphan, who should have died as a teenager, then again in his twenties, but became a werewolf, or vampire, or some combination of the two, I can't be certain, I'm no zoologist. Anyways, as I was saying, our main character had precisely what he wanted out of life for all of one day, half a day really, before it was all taken away from him. Torn from him, like wax from a nasty bikini line.

If you're not familiar with my stories, let me just say, bits of them might seem fictional to you. The reason being, I tend to look in places that most people won't, so, I see what they don't. It really is that simple, though I must warn you, and so I am, if you choose to seek out the things that go bump in the night, if your choice is to see the things that live in the corner of your eye, you will find them, rather, they'll find you.

Some of the stories feel familiar to me, and they are the ones that I like to share. I feel for Collin and his battles. His reality was turned upside down without much warning. His distinction between fact and fiction was annihilated in a dreamlike moment, and that, I think, is another connection I've made with the young man. I've had a few moments that I'd consider epiphanies. One's worldview can morph in the moment that it takes to admit that they were wrong. And that moment can make a lifelong adjustment in one's calibrations.

If a fictional character or event can become real in a rational mind, then I submit that people, things and events that were and are real could become fiction in that same rational mind. Fact and fiction, what is real to the mind is fact, and what is fiction to that mind cannot exist. Perspective is key to understanding, and since they, perspectives that is, are as unusual as we are, and as numerous, who really knows what separates fact from fiction.

Is it popular consent that decides the norm? Is it the masses that dictate what is and is not acceptable? If so, it should be pointed out that it is the masses who have historically bought into propaganda. It is the masses who are targeted by conspiracies, and so, as you must let me tell the stories, I must let you decide what can and cannot exist outside of your perspective, in the corner of your eye.

We begin this chapter of Collin's life on the night that decided his fate. He and two other bag men, his only friends for the past few years, are out on a job. They are killing a man and anyone with him. They don't know who the man is, or why his life was up for termination. They are simply following orders, which, if not followed through with, would more than likely result with their own necks being propped up on the chopping block.

This book is dedicated to all that which unites us, reminding us that it is life itself which binds us, and that to know oneself is to understand every self.

Look to each other and see yourselves…but, keep an eye out for psychos.

Enjoy.

1

Eric Thibeault sat nervously behind the wheel of an idling 1983 Buick Riviera. The car's dark blue paint dulled by years of sitting in the sun gave it a flat look, dull and flat, much like the eyes of the junky driving it. The cigarette he was sucking on had an inch long heater, and the drenched butt pretty well killed it's smokability. He drew on the damp butt again, realized that it was pooched, and tossed it out the window with a jittery hand. Eric lit another smoke, his eyes darting from the lighter's flame to the apartment building entrance that he was parked across from. He took a long haul on the new cigarette, killing it on the first drag. He choked on the smoke and coughed violently, launching spittle and phlegm into the windshield and all over the dashboard.

"Come on!" Eric spat as he threw his fresh smoke out the window. It found itself on the concrete with four other partially smoked, soggy butts. He was about to light another one, and felt sick immediately at the thought of it. But a little coke on the other hand, would fix him up perfectly. He reached into his jacket pocket and pulled out a small Russian doll. He'd stolen the carving from a friend's home when he was a boy, some twenty years earlier. His schoolmate had invited him over, they'd played a while, then his buddy showed him the doll, twisting the head, pulling it off and revealing another inside. How many dolls were hidden under the first, Eric couldn't remember, but there must have been a dozen. When Eric saw the smallest one opened, and empty, he simply needed to have it. He didn't even make an attempt to sneak it out. As his little friend smiled proudly and said, "isn't it neat?," Eric nodded, grabbed the little Russian doll, got up, and walked out of the stunned boy's house.

The moment Eric's shaky fingers found the coke holder, he heard what he'd been waiting for. It was faint, but he knew instantly that it was a gunshot. Within seconds, two more muffled shots popped, and Eric's stomach leaped. He'd been waiting for it, but now that it was here, the anticipation was brutal. He hated being the driver. The wait was always excruciatingly long, especially after gunfire.

He was gritting and grinding his teeth. He wanted to drive off, now. "Fuck 'em," he mumbled. "They're dead, I'm next...this sucks!"

But no, if there was a chance that they were still alive, and he bailed on them, again, it would mean a horribly painful end to his pathetic existence. If he turned up at Hooch's without Collin and Mac, he was dead.

Eric's heart stopped when he heard the first siren half a minute later. He broke out into a cold sweat. "God I hate being sober," he hissed through his teeth.

A shaky hand shifted the beat up Riviera into drive. Eric

cranked the wheel to the left, checked his blind spot, and began to pull out of the getaway car's parking spot, but he suddenly threw it back into park, grinding the heavy car to a jerky and noisy stop. He scratched at his neck while cursing under his breath. He pounded his tiny fists on the steering wheel, accidentally honking the horn. "Come on...hurry the fuck up!" he moaned, vibrating in the drivers seat, his eyes darting all about aimlessly, looking for movement, or anything that could be a good enough reason to flee.

Eric tried to remember the sound of the gun that he'd heard. He wondered if all the shots were the same gun. The sirens were still screaming, and he was pretty sure that they were coming his way. Eric looked up at the apartment building and noticed that a lot of people were at their windows and on their balconies. He could feel their eyes on him. Once again the car was shifted into drive, but this time there was no going back. Eric pulled out into the one way street, and stepped on the gas.

∞

Mac burst through the doors like a man possessed. His feet barely met the concrete as he downed the steps three at a time. He stumbled when he hit the sidewalk, and halted in the grip of a panic attack. He had nowhere to go. The car was supposed to be right in front of him. The profanities were about to fly when Mac felt a hand squeeze his shoulder.

"Don't lose it," said Collin calmly, but Mac could hear the anger that carried the words.

"Sirens," Mac pointed out.

"Yeah, they might not be for us, but I don't think we should wait to find out," said Collin as he looked over at his junky friend, trying to gauge his frame of mind. "Look at me buddy. Take a deep breath...good...we've got a minute...just breath, stay focused."

"Sure man, I'll focus on killing that fuckin' douche. I'm gonna kill him." Spat Mac as he displayed his freakout dance, hands swiping at the air, feet kicking at nothing.

Collin had been surveying his surroundings. The only people that he could see were in the park across the street. One vehicle had passed since they'd exited the apartment building. Another one, a Jeep Cherokee was approaching them, and it was slowing down, with the driver eyeing the spot where Eric, the MIA junky should've been parked, ready and waiting.

"Mac," Collin said, "we're gonna need that Jeep. Stay cool, looks like he's gonna park."

"In our spot," Mac protested.

"Stay cool, don't spook him. Wait till he's parked and the engine is off, ok? Come at him from his blind spot, and I'll get the passenger side," directed Collin.

"Got'cha," said Mac as he set off towards the Jeep.

"Stay cool partner," Collin reminded his friend, the sociopath.

Mac didn't look back. His limited attention was focused on the task at hand, and Collin was more than a little worried that things were about to get even uglier than they needed to.

The Jeep was backing into the parking spot, and the driver hadn't noticed the tall skinny unkempt figure that was approaching his door. And he hadn't yet seen Collin, the hairless brick-house that was now stepping onto the curb one vehicle behind his. He didn't see Mac reach for his door handle, or hear Collin bark "Wait!" but he did hear and sense his door open the instant that it did. He hit the brakes and turned to see a tall scraggly man with long hair and a goatee reaching for him with one hand, and the other closefisted, cocked, and about to strike.

The driver was startled, but not to the point of confusion. His reaction was to let off the brakes and step on the gas. The Jeep lurched backwards, it's open door knocking the carjacker sprawling to the oil stained asphalt in mid punch. The Jeep crashed to a halt, crumpling the hood and bumper of the sedan parked behind it. Then, the driver slapped the Jeep into gear and pulled away, squawking the tires and nearly running over Mac's right shoulder and arm.

Collin had the chance to try the passenger side doors, but they were locked, and there was nothing that he could do but watch as the Jeep sped away. The sirens were fast approaching, and the only thing that he could think of doing now was to run back into the apartment building, and try to find a way to hide from the police. But Collin didn't like that idea. The cops would canvas, and would eventually find them. There were eyes everywhere now.

"Get your ass up!" Collin growled at an embarrassed Mac. "Seriously, what the fuck is wrong with you?"

"Wasn't my fault," Mac said as he got to his feet. "Come on man, fucker almost killed me."

"Yeah, well, you just screwed us both Mac," said Collin.

"Wasn't my..."

"Shut up!" snapped Collin, as he flicked Mac's forehead with a practised finger. He was cool under pressure. He didn't panic, which is mostly what made him good at his job. Right now, he was thinking of himself. Something he'd been doing more and more of lately. He knew that Mac would make an arrest impossible. They'd both be shot down while Mac flung insults at the police. Mac had a gun too, that was bad, he'd surely use it.

"We're going to have to split up Mac. Keep calm, head across the park...meet me at Hooch's in two hours," Collin advised. "And get rid of your gun, discreetly, got it?"

Mac nodded, then frowned, showing his doubt for Collin's plan. And just as he was about to give Collin a piece of his mind, the '83 Buick Riviera came screeching to a stop a couple of feet from them. Eric was at the wheel, his bloodshot eyes bulging from their sockets.

"Come on! Hurry the fuck up!" yelled Eric through an open window.

Collin opened the door, pushed the seat's backrest forward and hopped in the back. Mac took the front seat, slamming the door as the car began its getaway. They made it two car lengths before the shouting began. The car, which drove like a boat, swerved, scraping alongside the parked cars that lined the street.

"Where did you go, you stupid fuckstick?!" shouted Mac.

"What the hell took you guys so long man? Just leave me here...I was freakin' out here man!" said Eric, like it was a valid argument.

"What?!! All you had to do was sit here and wait, you chickenshit fucktard...we're gonna..."

"Shut up!" Intervened Collin. "Watch your driving for Christ's sake, slow down Eric."

"Yeah!" shouted Mac, "and what the fuck..."

"I said shut up! Let him drive!" bellowed Collin. This was not the time or place to resolve anything. Eric would get his, there was no doubt about that much. Hooch had made it pretty clear that the ice was thin for the two dildos in the front seats. For now, his task was to get them to the garage in one piece.

They were turning right, off of the apartment building's street two blocks up from it when the first cruiser came flying around a corner three blocks back. It stopped in front of the building, then two more cars showed up on the scene before Collin's view of them was cut off by a brick barber shop.

Traffic was light, thankfully, and the three amigos had no difficulties in making it to the freeway. Tensions were high in the car but the fading sound of the sirens allowed them to relax a little. It was Eric who broke the silence.

"Collin, I'm sorry man...it was, I mean..."

"It's behind us, drop it, concentrate on the road, slow down," Collin interrupted.

"Wait!" pleaded Mac. "I wanna know why the fuck he took off. Bullshit man, what kinda..."

"Just shut it!" scowled Collin. "I don't want to hear another word outta either of you, unless you're down with me breaking your necks."

A minute later, Eric almost missed their off-ramp. He couldn't help checking his rear-view mirror, where he saw so much contained anger. He thought that he could feel it radiating against the back of his neck. He only looked back at the road because Collin met his gaze in the mirror. It was almost too late. Eric jerked at the wheel to get into the lane that he should have been in, but the car was going too fast. He hit the brakes, and steered the big steel car through a great recovery. The problem was that a recovery was required, especially when a speed trap was set up under that particular ramp.

"Damn! That was a close one," sighed Eric as he tried to swallow his heart back into place.

"Yeah, what the fuck man? There's nobody else on the road...how could you miss the turn off?" whined Mac.

"Uh, I dunno," said Eric as he glanced into the rear-view to see Collin looking right back.

"Neither one of you saw the cop back there, did you?" asked Collin, already knowing the answer.

Eric and Mac looked at each other, the same puzzled expression on their faces. And, as if on cue, they both replied, "What cop?"

"He was on the side of the road, under the ramp, with a radar gun. He's gonna be on us any minute. Just try to get to the garage, don't stop," ordered Collin.

"How you know the cop's coming after us? I don't see nothin'...nothin'," offered Mac.

"I can feel it Mackenzie, that's how." answered Collin.

"Nah, I didn't see him either...and if he was parked under the ramp, then he'd hav'ta go the wrong way on the freeway to get after us, right? Cops can't do that man." stated Eric.

"Yeah," Mac agreed. "Pigs can't turn left in a chase, and they can't go the wrong way on the highway neither...I've heard that."

"Right!" growled Collin from the backseat. "And they can't speed, or hurt anyone, cause that would be against the law. Yeah, sure thing."

Eric was about to defend himself and his best bud, but before he could lock eyes with baldy, he saw the flashing lights in the distance behind them. They were way back there, in the dark, but they were coming."

"Shit!", the word escaped Eric's dry lips.

Without turning to look, Collin said, "told you."

"Just keep going? To the garage?" asked Eric.

Collin thought about it for a moment. They were heading for some storage units on highway 9. That's where the Buick was stored when it wasn't being used. Collin was thinking that he could hide the patrol car in a storage unit, but it would most likely have a tracking system. And the cop would be calling all of this in, giving his brothers a rough idea of where he'd be if Collin let the chase go as far as their destination. The police would surely sweep the area too. That would be very bad considering what the storage units contained. No, he'd have to get rid of the cop now.

"Turn off the car." said Collin.

"Do what now?" Eric asked hesitantly.

"Put the car in neutral, turn it off, and stop, in the middle of the road. I'll take care of this." Collin said confidently.

"Okalydoke," said Eric. He shifted the car into neutral, turned it off, and looked out at an unlit highway. All the lights in the car were off. He could hear the tires on the asphalt, but other than that, the car was silent as it coasted along. Eric stepped on the brakes and brought the car to a full stop in the middle of the highway, just as requested.

Collin tapped Mac on the shoulder, "let me out."

2

The cop standing on the side of the road holding the radar gun was already heading back to his car to pursue when he heard the speeding Buick's tires squawk. He looked over his shoulder in time to see the car veer onto the off-ramp, fishtailing out of view.

Officer Scott breathed deeply as he tried to keep the effects of adrenaline in check. He made sure that no vehicles were coming his way, then proceeded to the ramp. He didn't call anything in until he'd gotten up the ramp, and up to speed. He could see the tail lights up ahead. There was no way that boat was going to outrun him.

The chatter over the radio was helping to keep his adrenal gland pumping. A man who'd escaped an attempted car jacking had given a description of a man and the car that had picked him up. There had also been gunshots heard only moments earlier. When officer Scott had seen that Buick, he'd felt it in his gut immediately. He just knew that it was bad news. From the sounds of it, a single highway infraction was about to turn into apprehending a couple of cold blooded killers.

Officer Scott wasn't sure what to think when he saw the break lights disappear. It didn't look like the vehicle had turned. Maybe they blew a tire, or hit the ditch...it was all over the road after all. It was difficult for him to gauge exactly where it was up ahead that the car had disappeared. Maybe a kilometer, maybe less. He kept up his speed for half a kilometer, then let off the gas, letting the car coast. He couldn't see the Buick anywhere. He decided that it was a job for the spotlight. He flicked a switch, turning the bright light on, but it was facing his left. He was about to redirect the light when he saw it from the corner of his eye. The Buick's reflector gave away it's position...dead ahead, forty yards. He slammed on the brakes, and they pushed back in pulses. He pushed harder, and the tires screamed while the patrol car slid, and skidded to a stop within feet of the Buick.

Officer Scott was shaken, but he managed not to miss a beat. He called in his location, gave the vehicle description and plate number. He was also able to confirm a driver and one passenger. He could see their silhouettes sitting, talking, and somewhat heatedly from the looks of it. He asked for backup, and was told that they were a few minutes out. So he exited his unit, pulled his firearm, and hoped for a sign of aggression.

He called out to them as he approached, "Get your hands on the dashboard, where I can see them, now, both of you...now!"

They both did as he asked. Officer Scott shone his flashlight on the backseat, nothing there. He moved closer to the driver who seemed very restless. He was practically vibrating in his seat. His hands were a blur as his fingers were hammering out some kind of hypersonic drum solo.

"You ok there buddy? A few too many coffees today I bet eh? You tweekin' fella?" Officer Scott asked with a grin. The driver's hands stopped, but then his body started rocking back and forth in his seat while the cop tore into him about his driving, and being a punk.

"Ok, tell ya what boys. You're fucked, you know it...so just relax, ok...just take it easy," he said as he shone the light from one face to the other. And that was when he heard his words being repeated from right behind him.

"Take it easy," it barely registered with him at first, but it all clicked a moment later when he felt the muzzle press into the small of his back, and strong fingers wrapping around his throat.

∞

Collin opened the passenger door and pushed the seat forward, hard, pushing Mac's face into the windshield. He hopped into the back and let the seat go. It fell with a bang under Mac's weight, whose head snapped back. His hands flew to his neck and he cursed.

"Let's go!" Collin barked.

Eric stomped on the gas and asked, "the cop dead?"

"No," replied Collin.

"What! Why not?!" snarled Eric.

"Really," said Collin, "where, other than prison do cop-killers get respect? You plannin' on goin' to prison fucknuts?"

Eric glared into the rear-view, internally cursing the smug prick that was glaring right back at him. Eric would've killed that cop in an instant had he gotten the chance. He couldn't believe that Collin just let the pig go. What a pussy. And if he didn't have all those muscles, he'd tell him so too.

"Right on," said Mac, "I can't wait for today to be over." He'd spotted the huge advertising sign up ahead, 'Sam's Bait Shop, Guns, Bows and Ammo', 10 km ahead on the right,' it said. The sign meant that their destination was just around the next bend.

Once they got there, things went smoothly enough. Mac got

out of the Buick, unlocked a padlock, and raised the garage door. Eric shut the car off, and left it in neutral. Collin wiped down the interior of the Riviera and looked for anything that might be laying around. He then did a quick once over of the vehicle's door handles, trunk, and spots that he thought someone might have touched. Once satisfied, he moved to the back of the car.

"Come on Mac, help me push...Eric, man the wheel would ya...and use your gloves," ordered Collin.

Eric steered the Buick into the makeshift garage through the open driver's window. He let out a 'whoa' when they'd run out of room, waited for the car to stop, then slapped the transmission into park.

"Good work men," offered Collin, hoping that he could set a more positive tone for the rest of the evening. "Good work, lock it up, let's go get paid."

∞

3

Every trade, business and profession employs those who produce, the bureaucrats who govern them, and hopefully keep them employed, and those who profit from the groups who do the toiling. Such is the model that we're meant to respect. Workers, management, and profiteers. Maintain profits by any means, whether the products or services are required or not, as needs can always be invented. We make crap for the most part, crap that will soon be scrap, and replaced by another shiny turd.

Capitalism is what they call it. Not many understood what that word really meant better than the thin man sitting in a big chair in a dark room. He's talking on the phone, his name is Hamilton. He is scrupulous, but easily sets his ideals aside while fulfilling his role as a facilitator, and intermediary of sorts, between labourers and profiteers. Hamilton could make anything happen, because he understood very well the key principles of capitalism and enterprise.

There were only three as far as Hamilton was concerned. When requiring a thing or service, the first, and usually only step required was payment, or an offer to pay. Most transactions were that simple. If re-numeration or service of equal value could not persuade ones bedfellows, then threats and force were principles number two and three. Hamilton had a great advantage within this system, as principle number three came easily to him. You see, he fears no man, and he has the wisdom of experience on his side.

"I couldn't agree with you more," he said into the antique phone. He watched his octopus dancing around in it's aquarium as he listened to the voice at the other end of the line.

"Agreed, I think he's our man. I'll bring him in slowly...I'll have a few chats with him, don't worry," Hamilton implored.

"No, he's loyal to them, but I think he'll see the big picture. Give him a couple days and he'll appreciate the opportunity, I'm sure of it," he said confidently.

One hell of an opportunity, Hamilton thought as he admired the forest that was painted on the wall to his left. There wasn't a single window on one of the four, two thousand square foot floors that were his second home. No windows, instead, massive murals engulfing entire walls, and in some places spreading to the ceilings. Cityscapes, mountain ranges, desert and jungle sunsets, a farm. Hamilton particularly enjoyed the forest scene. If he stared at it long enough, he'd often see creatures in the fauna, and birds in the trees. The lava lamp helped give life to the effect.

"Ya, Friday makes sense to me. They'll be up for a good time.

They might be too stupid to find the place without Collin," Hamilton said as he surveyed the woods again for activity.

"No, I'll find something for him, maybe even have him over here. We'll see how things go tomorrow," he said into the phone's brass handle.

One of the monitors on the wall to Hamilton's right caught his attention. A cop car was pulling into the entrance to his parking lot. Hamilton checked the clock, the cruiser was right on time.

"Absolutely Stephan," Hamilton said, "I'll mentor him if you're not into it, I'm confident he's a good fit...yes, the other two are yours, put them to work, don't, I couldn't care less. Listen, I have to let you go, boys in blue are here. Be well my friend, I'll see you this weekend."

Hamilton placed the phone on it's cradle. He checked his monitors for his foot soldiers. They were on the third floor, driving up the final ramp to the fourth floor. Hamilton could come and go from any floor, but his visitors could only gain access via the top. There was a steel door that opened outwards, then a steel cage that could only be opened the old fashioned way, with a key.

Hamilton's office/second home was impressive to say the least. Ingenious as well. No one using the parking garage would even consider that a man was housed in a concealed fortress where they stored their car for the day. Even those who were aware and allowed to enter only ever saw the top floor. They might have wondered, but they couldn't know for sure if all the levels were a part of his hideout.

Hamilton made his way to the cage where he waited a minute for the two officer's knock. When it came, he pushed a button that was hidden, disguised as a piece of another mural. The outer door's latch fell with a loud thud, and a uniformed figure opened it all the way as it stepped into the cage. Once the second was in, the door was closed and latched behind them.

"Good morning," greeted Hamilton.

"Mornin' H," replied the officers.

"Kato, Rowan," said H, slipping a key into the cage's lock, "please have good news for me."

Hamilton led them to his study, the forest room, while Rowan brought him up to speed on a case they'd been following.

"They stopped, in the middle of the highway?" asked Hamilton.

"Yeah," confirmed Rowan. "Officer Scott didn't see the car till he was on top of it."

Hamilton thought about it, and decided that it must have been Collin's idea. He walked over to a hidden panel in the forest. He pushed on a corner and it popped open, revealing a small built-in fridge. He grabbed two small white bottles, like old-fashioned wide mouthed milk bottles, then closed the fridge and offered them to Rowan and Kato, who accepted and drank from them eagerly.

"Yeah," continued Rowan, " so, he slams on the brakes, stops inches from the car...said he almost shat himself. Anyways, he's shooken up a little, thought he'd lost them, right. He calls it in, runs the plates...he sees two people in the car, he's heard the radio chatter, and he's pretty sure these are the perps all that chatter's about. Oh, when he calls it in, he's told backup is on it's way, three or four minutes tops. So, all Scott has to do is sit tight for a few minutes, but he decides to confront them. He's pissed, his balls are still in his stomach, right. He pulled his gun before approaching the car, a month worth of paperwork, but whatever, he thought the situation called for it. He doesn't see anything in the car or on them, they've got their hands on the dash, and he starts provoking them, giving them the second degree, trying to get a reaction I'd bet. He notices the driver's pretty twitchy and starts in on him, tells him to relax, he's caught, there's nothing to worry about anymore, just let go, sit back and relax. And, well, that's when someone, your Collin, grabbed him. Scott says he didn't sense a thing, just heard a whisper, felt a gun against his spine and a hand at his throat. Said it was soft, but strong as hell, I thought that was funny. Anyways, he was immobilized before he understood what'd happened."

"You observed all of this yourself?" asked Hamilton.

"Yes," said Rowan.

"He was pretty smooth then. And, he didn't kill the officer?" asked Hamilton.

"Yeah, he was smooth. Didn't look to me like he was even trying to be sneaky. Standing straight up, just walked outta the bush, right up to Scott. He was, uh, pressed for time, and made it look easy. And Scott says he never saw the guy's face. Said he was on his tippy toes the whole time. Collin practically carried him by the throat through the ditch and into the trees," said

Rowan.

"What? Why didn't he just knock the poor guy out, put him in his own trunk?" asked Hamilton.

"Yeah, well, it surprised me too...Scott thought he was dead for sure. Figured he'd take one in the head and they'd take his cruiser. But nope, Collin slams him up against a tree, and tells him to hook his left leg around it. So he does...then Collin tells him to hook his left foot behind his right knee. Now, he has to lift his right foot, eh, but it's no problem, he's being held off the ground by the back of the neck. So, Scott tosses his right leg over his left foot," Rowan took another swig, draining the bottle. He chuckled a little, then added, "then the guy tells him to hook his right foot around the base of the tree. He tries, but can't quite reach it, so, Collin did it for him. Just grabbed his foot, pulled it around the tree, and pushed his body down to the ground. Now he's sitting on top of his right foot, and his knees are about to pop, but Collin pushes down on him some more, sits him right in the dirt...you shoulda heard him whining. Then, he wishes him a good night and walks away. He drops Scott's gun about six feet from him, and just keeps walking."

"Effective manner of subduing, I'm sure, a leg lock with a tree, but, why go through all the trouble?" asked Hamilton.

"Time," said Kato.

Hamilton nodded, his eyes asking for more.

"Scott was on their ass, he had to be dealt with" explained Kato, "by taking him out, and strapping him to a tree, he gained more time than he lost. The next units would stop, they'd hear

Scott yelling and spend a couple minutes finding him and getting him on his feet, and likely hear his story. I think it was smart. If he'd been in the trunk, the first unit would of stuck with him, but the second would have given chase immediately, without having to locate their fallen brother."

"He's pretty cool under pressure," added Rowan, "but none of it was really necessary. He could of knocked Scott out, backup didn't show up for a good five minutes."

"Fair enough," said Hamilton, "I've heard what I needed to, thank you. Now, tell me, how are things on a day to day basis? How are we getting along?"

Rowan and Kato glanced at each other, Rowan nodded, and Kato spoke, "couldn't be easier, really. Everything is under control. I gotta say though, Sir, we're looking forward to retirement."

"Understood. So many better things that you could be doing with your time. It'll come gentlemen, be patient, another month or so, we'll have some fresh blood in training, and you'll be on your way to bigger and better things. We must all earn our stripes. I've been doing this a long, long time. Many of us have. Your sacrifice has and will always be appreciated." said Hamilton firmly.

"Of course, we get it," said Kato, "it's just that, it's almost been 20 years. I don't, we don't really feel like we're pretending anymore. It'll be nice to get away from thinking like cops, that's all."

Hamilton laughed at this. "Well, Kato, let me tell you

something. For all intensive purposes, you are cops, so that's a good thing. We all have our roles to play. I don't have to remind you of all the benefits that you've inherited, do I?

"No H, it just gets a little mundane. It can be tedious," replied Kato, looking at the floor.

"Yes, I am aware," said Hamilton, "Listen, you know how our system is set up. There's always been a delicate balance. I'd love to have a more philosophical sit down with you, but I do have other things to attend to, I apologize."

"That's ok," interjected Rowan, "We gotta get back out there anyways. Serve and protect and all that good stuff."

"Another day in paradise," Hamilton smiled. "Just remember who you're serving and protecting, we're counting on each other my friends."

Hamilton then led the police officers back towards the cage. He unlocked it, took the little white bottles from his visitors, then closed the gate door behind them while they said their farewells. Hamilton engaged the outer door's lock and waved to Kato and Rowan as they stepped back into their roles as public servants.

∞

4

The drive back to town from the storage units had been uneventful. Eric drove, Mac sat up front with him, and Collin sat quietly in the back, listening to his junky buddies exchange ideas on how they could spend their pay. Collin already knew what he needed the money for. He was young, but was already planning for his retirement, whereas, from the sounds of it, Eric and Mac would be broke again by the end of the week.

When they got to Hooch's pool hall, Eric pulled the car around back and parked in the handicap parking spot. They went in through the back door, and headed for Hooch's office. He had gotten his nickname as a teenager. He was not an attractive man, and had been dubbed Hooch for resembling a dog by the same name that appeared in a movie years earlier.

Now in his early forties, he was balding, his jowls hung low, and seemed to bleed into his massive double chin, which ballooned from ear to ear. It was his sagging eyes that mostly gave him the look of a dog though. A thick watery red mass under each eye which made it difficult for most people to lock gazes with him, as their own eyes would tend to water.

Hooch had seen the boys arrive on his monitors. He yelled at them to enter just as Collin was about to knock on the door. Collin came through the door first, he greeted Hooch with a nod, then moved to a corner of the room while Eric and Mac took the only two chairs.

"Show me da money," mused Eric as he reached out with an open palm.

"Shut the fuck up," mumbled Hooch.

"Yeah, yeah, I was just fu.."

"I said SHUT UP! You can't do nothin' right, can you? Just sit there, and be quiet, GOT IT!" bellowed the annoyed fat man. "Now," Hooch said calmly, "I hear you twits almost got yourselves caught. Got two descriptions, and the car was made too."

"Yeah," said Mac, "but we're here, the job..."

"Shuttin' the fuck up goes for you too," growled Hooch, with a fat finger pointed at Mac's mouth.

"Collin," Hooch said, focusing his attention on the hairless man in the corner, "what happened?"

Collin took a moment to reflect, then said, "Everything went off without a hitch. Cops turned up sooner than expected, and, uh, we had to get a little creative."

"Yeah, sure...tell me, you like having your driver take off on ya when you're in the middle of a fuckin' job?" asked Hooch as his eyes shifted to Eric who was chewing at his lips and rocking back and forth in his chair.

Collin again took a moment to answer, then said, "I'm sure he had a good reason...and he didn't go far. He picked us up, we got away."

Eric was now nodding profusely in agreement, and his feet were playing a couple of invisible kick drums, double time.

"That's some pretty weak shit right there man," said Hooch flatly. "useless if you ask me, god damn liability," he added.

"Come on man," Eric started, with Hooch instantly cutting him down with a glare. Eric was about to get an earful, when a ringing phone diffused the verbal assault. It was a white phone, sitting on a shelf behind Hooch. The ugly fat man jumped slightly in his seat when he realized which phone was sounding. He didn't like that phone much, as he never had any input in white phone matters. He'd broken out in a sweat, and had gone pale too. That phone only rang a couple of times a year, but he thought about it every day, and he was always scared shitless that it might ring.

Hooch held up a hand, signalling 'one moment,' as his eyes darted about the room like a caged animal's might. He quickly realized though, that there was no choice here, other than picking up the ringing phone, and saying hello. He swivelled in his chair, rubbing his hands together, grabbed the receiver, held it to his ear and said it, "Hello?"

Hooch listened for a long moment, then said, "uh, yeah, in fact, they're right here in front of me." He listened intently again, his eyes falling on Eric, then on Mac, back and forth from one tool to the other. "Understood," he said into the phone, "yes, he's here too," Hooch confirmed as his gaze moved to Collin.

"Ok, not a problem, Yessir, tomorrow, 9pm, the parking lot, 4th floor. And, uh, Friday, the farm. Did I miss anything?" asked Hooch politely, hoping that this conversation would soon be over, and he was very relieved when it turned out to be. He slowly replaced the receiver on it's pedestal, and turned to face his audience.

"Uh, good news fellas," he said. "Collin, you can leave now, head home, or, whatever it is you do. I've got a big job for these two."

Hooch scribbled an address on a piece of paper, then held it out in Collin's direction. Mac reached for it, thinking that he could simply pass it over, but Hooch pulled his hand back, shook his head, and held out the piece of paper again, for Collin to collect.

"Tomorrow, 9pm, be there, and don't be late, got it?" Hooch spoke slowly, emphasizing each syllable, and Collin understood immediately that this was an important matter.

Collin stepped out of the corner, not wanting to accept the task, but he took the address from the fat sweaty man. It read 912 Dundas, parking garage, 4th floor.

"Sounds a little sketchy," remarked Collin. "I don't think I like us being on separate jobs Hooch...who's gonna have my back on this one?"

"You don't need anyone slick. Just gonna have a little sit-down, as far as I know. That call was from your, uh, fairy god-father, capiche? Looks like you've caught the right people's attention," said Hooch.

"Yeah, I don't like it Matthew," said Collin to Hooch, who rarely heard his real name anymore, and was pleasantly surprised to hear it now. He liked Collin, he was respectful and thoughtful, and he could be trusted. He had his head screwed on right, unlike the other two.

"I hear ya guy, but there's nothing to worry about, ok?" reassured Hooch.

"Yeah, so why were you so scared of that phone? You always get nervous when talking to nice, well meaning folk?" asked Collin.

"Well, let's call it performance anxiety, Ok? When that phone rings, it means big jobs, and big pay. Nice and well meaning has nothing to do with anything, you're right about that," Hooch locked eyes with Eric, then Mac, then back and forth again for effect. "Big jobs, big pay...but if you fuck up, you get stupid...you're dead. Plain and simple." Hooch looked to Collin, "You think these two can manage a pick-up without you? I have my doubts."

"I have no clue why I wouldn't be going with them. Doesn't make sense to me either...sorry guys, no disrespect meant," Collin said to Eric and Mac, who weren't even really paying attention anymore.

Hooch sat back in his chair and thought on it while Eric twitched, and Mac's eyes glazed over with daydreams of paydays, drugs, and all the little Asian girls that he'd be able to afford.

"It's not my call Collin," said Hooch as a matter of factly. "It's not your call either. If the job was too big for these two dildos, they wouldn't be going, that's it, that's all. You sir, need to focus on getting your ass to that meeting and making a good impression, cool?"

"Cool. I'll make the meeting," stated Collin, "but if I don't like what I hear, and I think the 'dildos' need me, I'm going with them."

Hooch slumped forward, and his chair creaked under his weight, "Yeah, I wouldn't do that if I were you...but, I'm not you, am I? If I was you, I'd be as happy as a paedophile on a deserted island with the mini-pops, got it?"

"I don't like it. Who am I going to meet?" inquired Collin.

"I don't know man! This is way over my head. I have no idea how he knew who you guys are," said Hooch, motioning over his shoulder with a thumb towards the white phone, "or how he knew to find you here. Frankly, I don't care to know, trust me, this is way over my head. Just go to the garage, listen to what has to be said, and decide for yourself what you're gonna do, Ok?"

"Any idea what's going to be expected of me?" asked Collin.

"I wish I knew man. I really do," admitted Hooch, "Now get outta here so I can give your friends here the details of their job."

"Sure thing," said Collin. Then he stepped between his seated buddies. He looked at each of them, then at Hooch, and kept the pose until Hooch asked, "Can I help you? The door's right there."

"I haven't been paid," said Collin with a crooked smile on his face.

Hooch slapped a meaty, slick palm to his forehead with a loud smack. "Sorry...got my mind on other things," he said while rubbing a temple. He withdrew three envelopes from his desk drawer. He handed one to Collin, and said, "now, get the fuck outta here, Ok?"

Collin opened his envelope, checked that it's contents were satisfactory, and slipped it into his jacket pocket. "Tomorrow, 9pm, Ok," he said to Hooch, then turned, looked to his comrades and told them to be good, that he'd call them tomorrow, and then he left.

There was an uncomfortable silence in the room now. It's occupants sat still, even Eric was motionless. Hooch was both happy and upset about the situation. Anyone he'd ever sent to the farm hadn't returned. That was a cause to celebrate with these two. But knowing that, and having to pay them seemed like such a waste.

"Be here," Hooch said while poking his index repeatedly on his desk, "at 7pm, Friday evening...the day after tomorrow." He slid each of their pays to the edge of his desk, where he hoped that they'd trust what he was about to tell them, being comforted by the wad of cash in their hands, and the promise of more to come.

"There's gonna be one of those new Camaro's here on Friday. You're going to take your new work vehicle on a little test drive. Be here at 7, sharp...be rested and ready for a three or four hour drive. Gonna make a pick-up, and get paid very well for it. Any questions? No? Good. Eric, when are you gonna be here?" asked Hooch pleasantly enough.

Eric thought about it for a minute, wondering if it might be a trick question. "Uh, 7pm, sharp, Friday."

"Mac," Hooch said, "how about you?"

"Yeah, 7pm man, Friday...sounds good man," replied Mac.

"Ok then" said Hooch, "this is your big chance boys, I know you're not going to fuck this up, right?"

"No way man," confirmed Mac.

"You can count on us Matthew," said Eric, immediately regretting having used Hooch's birth name. He saw a glint in the fat man's eye, and it didn't leave him with an easy feeling.

Eric was right, Hooch did not like hearing the word coming from him. He was happy to see the punk go, and that's what helped him keep his cool. "Good," he said, "that's good," he smiled, "now get out of here."

"Yeah, Ok Hooch," said Eric, attempting to redeem himself. "Have a good one eh, we'll see ya Friday, 7 sharp."

Hooch sat and watched the two dimwits while they made their way out of is office. It was a shame, he thought, that they each had twenty-five hundred of his money in their hands. That they'd have it blown by Friday night, and their odds of returning from the farm were slimmer than none.

"Gotta pay the reaper," he said out loud.

5

Collin was up early Thursday morning. He'd gone straight home after his meeting with Hooch, except for a stop at Toni's, where he got a medium pepperoni pizza to go. He ate the entire thing while watching a game-show where Japanese contestants were getting thrashed around by ludicrous obstacle courses. He laughed a great deal, and went to bed feeling rather carefree.

He drifted off the moment his head hit his pillow, but sleep was interrupted by a wandering mind. He hadn't given it much thought, but now, the idea of 'the farm' wouldn't leave him alone. Nothing had been said to put him on his guard, but the thought of Eric and Mac being given a job that would take them out into the country, on their own, well, that left a knot-like feeling in the pit of his stomach. And so, sleep did not come to him until he'd wasted a good hour over-thinking the unknown.

His entire night's rest was affected by dark dreams that he forced himself to wake from. Every time Collin would fall asleep, he'd wake up a few minutes later, check his alarm clock, roll over, and do it again. It continued till dawn, until finally, at 5:30am, he'd had enough. He got out of bed knowing full well that he'd had some twisted dreams, but he couldn't remember them. The only thing that stayed with him was a smell. A deep, dank scent like an old basement that hid within it something that was slowly rotting.

Even as Collin brewed some fresh coffee, it's aroma couldn't fully erase that pungent, moldy smell from his mind. He sipped on his first cup thinking about how he had a smell that he hadn't smelled stuck to the top of his mouth, soaked into his sinuses, and corrupting his taste buds. It wasn't until he checked his phone for weather details that the memory of the smell left him to enjoy his second cup of coffee.

Collin was usually up by 7am, but he wasn't sure what to do with himself this early on. He wound up making a big egg, bacon and hash-brown breakfast while watching some gorgeous women do aerobics on his t.v. He couldn't believe what they were wearing, or the poses that they were holding while the camera covered every nook and cranny. It was like early morning porn as far as he was concerned. And it was that notion that got him through the following hour. Once he'd eaten, he smoked a joint and pleasured himself to aerobics instructors on public television.

When he was done with loving himself, he had a shower, checked himself in the mirror for any stray hairs that he could shave. Alopecia had him bald from head to toe, but from time to time, patches of hair would pop up. Sometimes on his head, other times his eyebrows or beard would make an appearance. This morning though, there was nothing to shave, and Collin was a little disappointed.

By 8am he was walking onto a car lot a few blocks from his

place. He checked out a few used trucks at the back of the lot, then made his way to an area where they had some RV's and utility trailers. He pulled a small pad of paper and pen from his leather jacket, and jotted down a few prices and dimensions.

By 9am, Collin had walked a few miles down the road to another dealership where he did the same thing. He looked at trucks and trailers, and took notes. This lot had a few more Rv's, and he actually put up with a salesman long enough to check out a few of their interiors.

By 10am, he was working up a sweat at Moe's boxing gym where Collin trained almost daily. It was only a forty dollar a month fee, and he saw it as an investment in his health. He didn't spend much on anything else, just the basic sweat gear that any hobbyist might wear. He did however splurge a little on his shorts, which had two words embroidered into them at the waist, facing his opponents. They said quite simply, 'Your Mom'.

He had a regiment of cardio, weight training and six rounds of sparring, if anyone at the gym was able to last that long with Collin. He was fast, smooth, and hit like a jackhammer. He usually beat the shit out of three men during his six rounds. Today, only one other person was training, and after the first round, it was obvious that Stephan was not a trained boxer, but a natural brawler who was tough as nails.

The chiseled Frenchman took punches with a grin, and Collin tried to knock that smile off his face. He was thick in the chest and shoulders. He had a menacing black and silver goatee, with streaks of grey over his ears. His movement was slinky and staccato, and he made Collin work to land blows. During the fourth round, he asked Collin to pull his punches a little, or to stop hitting him so much. They both had a good laugh, and Collin decided to end his workout on a high note.

By noon, he was back in his three hundred square foot apartment eating a chicken salad and drinking his daily carrot and apple juice. Collin loved documentaries, and had seen some a few years back that claimed vegetable juice and a plant based diet could and would cure any ailment, from cancer to diabetes. When stated as simply as it had been, it was a difficult thing to believe. Cures through diet, not medicine was a revolutionary concept to him.

He tried to dismiss the documentaries claims, but couldn't help feel that they deserved some investigating. Collin understood the global model for what it was, a very few controlled the vast majority. He didn't have any difficulties postulating that some rich pharmaceutical interests could propagandize the food industry for profits, and if there was even a slim chance that this could be true, a change in diet could possibly be very beneficial.

Collin was a man that had been sick much of his life. He'd been on medications since childhood. One after another, new prescriptions would be offered that were meant to curb one symptom or another. So, when he saw that documentary about people who claimed drugs made everything worse, as the only thing that could heal a body was the body itself, Collin found himself wanting to believe it. The theory was that if fed the proper nutrients, in a digestible manner, the body would react by maintaining itself. It was too simple a concept to argue, and he'd never heard it before.

It was because of that want to believe that Collin made a lifestyle change, and was now living proof that you are what you eat. He'd bought a juicer, began eating raw organic vegetables, and within two months, his doctor was telling him there was something odd going on, because he didn't seem to be sick anymore. His liver was healthy, his blood looked great...it was a miracle, and they needed to determine which drug or combination of prescriptions it could all be attributed to.

Well, wouldn't you know it? When Collin explained his diet and it's purpose with great delight, and recounted how one by one, he'd stopped taking his drugs, his doctor was beside himself with disbelief. Dr. Swanson even brought in some of his peers to review the case, and hear what Collin had to say. They explained to him how he'd fallen victim to some less than honourable people. These scoundrels were killing people by gaining their trust through false hope, and profiting immensely from their naivety.

Collin had thought about their warnings, and had asked them how these scoundrels expected to profit by telling people to grow gardens. How much could they stand to make? When Collin compared the cost of fruits and vegetables to that of medications, it was fairly obvious who stood to make and/or lose profits in the health racket.

Collin only ever returned to see his doctor once since that visit. It was six months later, and it was to satisfy his curiosity. He'd felt better than ever, had lost fat and gained muscle and colour. His eyes were brighter and clarity of thought and focus were even brighter yet. When all results came back with flying colours, it was all Collin needed to hear to fully accept that he'd beaten his ailments.

He had one more to defeat though, his career. It's not easy for a sickly man to hold down a decent job. Miss a week or two here and there, and it's not long before a new career path is on the horizon. After one particularly long stint of unemployment, Collin had participated in a B&E with Eric and Mac, who had always been outcasts like himself, but had never bothered trying to make it legitimately either.

Years later, he was stuck. The trio had progressed from petty crime to shakedowns and killings. They'd confront other criminals after a job, and demand a stake in their activity. They were doing some mafia's dirty work through an old acquaintance. Hooch could be pretty cold, but he had money and was willing to part with it. That was all that mattered to Collin for a couple of years, but his ambitions and priorities had changed. He envisioned a new future for himself. He was going to leave, no ifs, ands or buts about it. He'd lost a part of himself in his career as a thug, and for a long while he thought it was his soul that he'd lost.

It was only a month ago that Collin realized what it really was. It was his anger. He didn't like hurting people anymore, not that he ever really enjoyed it, but he'd never minded it because his anger fed the violence. Without the anger that he'd always carried with him, he had nothing in him to drive the kinds of acts he'd often be expected to perform. It seemed to him that it was easier to do shitty things to others when his own future was bleak.

He had come to an impasse when he realized that he was no longer a victim. He was healthy, and he could do anything that he wanted. With a new-found respect for life, Collin was finding it more and more difficult to hurt people. And, whereas it was the complete opposite not long ago, Collin now found the most pathetic of people to be the ones that he wanted to protect the most. He felt a hundred times stronger than when he'd first become a bruiser. With his re-vitalizing diet and conditioning regime, Collin was often pitted against desperate souls who he could tear in half if he so desired. It was cruel, it was sad, and Collin wanted out. He wanted more beauty in his life.

Tonight's meeting was an unwanted surprise. He only needed a few more thousand dollars to get his new life off of the ground. Collin sat on his couch, drinking his carrot juice wondering just what could possibly be waiting for him on the fourth level of a parking garage downtown. The question sat heavily on his mind because of it's inopportune timing.

He checked his watch, 12:15 pm, nine hours to go, and he didn't have anything to do until then. He thought about going online, to look for some deals on fixtures for his project, but, there really wasn't much point to it, not until he had the money and was willing to part with it. He so wanted to take the plunge into another life altering pool of ideals, if he could just get out of here.

Collin checked his watch again, 12:17pm. He figured that he could work-out again, do some tai-chi, maybe follow up with a short nap, "sounds like a plan," he said aloud to himself.

The moment that he got to his feet, there was a knock on his door. When he looked through the eye hole and saw that it was Eric, his instinct was to pretend that he wasn't home. Collin looked through the hole again, and what he noticed this time was how haggard the junky looked. Collin sighed deeply, then unbolted the lock and opened the door.

"You look like shit," said Collin to Eric as he settled himself on Collin's couch.

"Really? I feel great!" smiled Eric.

"Yeah, you been up all night, haven't ya?" noted Collin.

"Oh, yeah man, good times, good times," mumbled Eric.

"Where's Mac?" asked Collin.

"Oh, yeah, he's still down at, uh, Miss Titty's...uh, Kitty's, Miss Kittys," said Eric.

"Ya, where you comin' from?" Collin asked.

"Oh, uh, I was just...I met this dude, eh. He had some mad wicked shit...I was rockin' out all night brother." said Eric.

"Rockin' huh. You mean, you shot up, and spent the night slobbering on yourself in an alley somewhere, right?" asked Collin.

"Can I have some toast man? Or something...maybe some water?" begged Eric.

"Ok, I'll make you some eggs and toast, and a cup o' Jo. But, you're not crashing here Eric, ok, got it?" pleaded Collin.

"Yeah, no, Ok man, sure thing...thanks big guy, savin' my ass here." grinned Eric, his eyes shut.

"No doubt, no doubt...you want your eggs scrambled?" Collin asked.

"Scrambled? I dunno. Do rich people eat scrambled eggs man?" Eric inquired.

"Rich people?" repeated Collin, assembling some ingredients and a pan.

"Yeah, ya man...or should I eat 'em sunny side up, or hard-boiled, ya know, sit the egg in that little stand thing, I could use my little egg spoon to tap it, eh, tap 'n crack the egg up." said Eric.

"I'm going to fry your egg up with a touch of olive oil Eric, eat it, like it, I don't give a shit," explained Collin.

Eric laughed, then continued with the egg talk, "yeah, no, that's awesome dude, I'm gonna love your eggs. I just meant, you know, we're going up in the world eh, movin' on up brotha. You got a big meeting tonight, and me and Mac got that new car and a big payday. Things're looking good bro, we should celebrate!" howled Eric.

"Yeah, going to a farm to pick something up. Not sure I'd run out and buy a Caddy just yet bud." said Collin.

"Whatever man, it's gonna be a slice," said Eric.

"Any idea where this farm is?" Collin asked.

"Naw, the fat fuck's gonna tell us where we're going tomorrow when we pick up the new car. Dude, new car, I said it like twenty times, and you haven't..."

"Yeah, yeah," interrupted Collin. "Ok Eric, new car eh? What'chou talkin' about?"

"Ha, you're a funny fuck, you know that? It's a brand spankin' new Camaro man. I hope it's yellow, eh, with those black stripes, and manual, I hope it's got a stick," said Eric.

"That would be pretty sweet m'man, no doubt. Better watch it though, right? I mean, a car like that turns heads. You'll be a heat-score, so you can't give 'em a reason to pull you over. Think about it, that's why we have the Corolla Eric." imparted Collin.

"Ya ya, fuck man, why you always bummin' me out? I'm excited big guy, we're gonna party like it's nineteen eighty...whatever the fuck year they partied...we're getting called up to the bigs Collin!" exclaimed Eric.

"Ok. That's fantastic. Here you are kingpin Eric, eggs, toast and coffee, just the way you like it...we had it flown in from a small country near the south pole where it's morning all day long, and they've mastered breakfast. Only the best for you from now on, your excellence," Collin joked while he curtsied and bowed. Then he placed Eric's meal on the coffee table in front of him.

Collin made himself a coffee while Eric devoured everything on the plate. By the time Collin had returned holding his cup, Eric was stretching out on the couch.

"No, come on man...what did I just say? I'll feed ya, but you're not crashing here! Come on," insisted Collin as he kicked the couch, "I'll call ya a cab, go home."

"I'm not crashing, just getting comfy bro," yawned Eric. "Just wanna chill a little," he trailed off.

"Hey! Don't you fuckin' fall asleep on me you little...Get up! Come on!" Collin barked at Eric while kicking the couch repeatedly, and contemplating hitting the little bastard instead.

But it was too late. Collin knew it too, and he was upset with himself for letting a thieving junky pass out on his couch. "Hey! Wake up! I'll take you out to your natural habitat if you don't get off my couch...eh, how about the alley...we can find some nice trash cans to hide you behind."

"Serenity now!" Collin shouted in a moment of utter frustration. He admitted to himself that he'd never be able to do such a thing to a friend, but also had to accept that his friend might rob him when he woke up. He'd no doubt cause some sort of completely unnecessary scene that could attract attention. The guy was a walking cop magnet, like a fly that was never far from it's prize...a big steaming pile of shit. Eric found it everywhere. And now, he was sleeping, in what could be considered a light coma, on Collin's couch, where, at some point, he'd wake up, and the shit would fly.

Wasn't much Collin could do about it now, nothing ethical anyways. He felt a little drained from dealing with Eric's intrusion. He decided that he too would get some rest and take a little nap. It was nearly 1pm. Collin went to his bed, set his phone's alarm clock for a two hour nap. Then he laid down for what was a sound and restful sleep.

It is a shame though, that not all manners of waking are as soothing as the sleep itself. Collin awoke to a crash and a yelp of pain. Eric had fallen off the couch and somehow managed to smash the coffee table's glass top in the process. Eric was awake, but only long enough to inspect his bloody hand, then he was back to snoring like a puppy.

"Nice way to wake up," said Collin loudly, "bloody junky and broken glass."

Collin checked his phone. There was three minutes left until his alarm went off. "Unreal," he said, practically shouting. He turned off the alarm and got busy cleaning up the broken glass from his floor. A coffee cup and plate had been broken in the crash as well, and Collin picked up all the tiny pieces while shaking his head and cursing the passed out freeloader that didn't stir once while his mess was dealt with.

When he was satisfied that he'd gotten all the little bits of his broken stuff, Collin took five minutes to check Eric's wound for glass, then clean and dress it with some gauze and vitamin E cream. He thought about lifting Eric back onto the couch, but decided that he'd do less damage from the floor.

Collin checked his watch again. Nearly six hours left till the 'movin on up' meeting. He decided it would be best spent keeping himself busy, and left his apartment for the gym. There would be at least ten guys there this time of day. Just might get himself a decent workout.

∞

6

Traffic was flowing like the the city's life-blood. People filled the sidewalks and criss-crossed the streets. Collin stood in front of the parking garage with his back to it, watching the coming and going of his fellow man as they finished up their work days and ran errands, or went out for dinner and drinks. He reflected on how disconnected he felt from them. He figured that it was because of a worldview that most people simply didn't share. He had a difficult time relating to people who strove to be what was popular, since he was never allowed to assimilate in the first place. He was never accepted into a group or society as a whole. He supposed that was why he felt distant from them. He'd earned the knowledge of self at an early age, and he was amused by those who were determined to be the same. To be, and think, and act like everyone else, the way they're supposed to, according to...and that's where Collin was stumped. Man had evolved into a fad.

He checked his watch, 8:50pm. Collin turned his back to the city sheeple and began his walk up the ramps and across the parking lot levels. And even though there were people driving down the ramps, and walking to their cars, Collin felt like he was the one being watched. Someone was eyeing him above all the other comers and goers. It was to be expected, he rationalized, after all, this was a white phone meeting, whatever that was.

There was at least one guard on each level from what Collin could see. No one in the pay booth though, that was automated. He wasn't sure if it was normal to see that many guards in a parking lot. Must be some high-rollers using it regularly enough to warrant this much muscle to deter thieves.

When he reached the top level, the fourth floor, he was once more under a darkening sky. Some stars were trying to reveal themselves through the dying light. Collin scanned the horizon, looking for the moon, but he saw none. Then he looked around for an indication of what he was supposed to do from here. He checked his watch, 8:56pm.

Collin walked across the parking lot, and looked out at the skyline, then down at the people and cars that were still coming and going. He turned and took in the parking lot, trying to figure out it's importance, and from his vantage point, he saw something that he found curious.

He was looking at a ten foot high wall in the middle of the parking lot. He was on the top level, why would a wall have to go that high? He took a few steps and saw that the wall continued around the corner. He looked down the ramp, and saw that all the walls were of the same dimension as up here. Collin wondered how much wasted space was built into this design. The walls must have been fifty feet long each. Over two thousand square feet wasted on every level. Curious. Then it hit him. He had a revelation. There was a roof. There's a building in there. Maybe one of the maintenance doors in the stairwell led to some dark mafia hideout. A room with a lamp, a table and some chairs, sitting on bloodstained floors.

When Collin rounded the next corner, he saw it. A door marked 'NO ADMITTANCE'. "As simple as that," he said to himself.

"What's your name?" asked a thick voice from behind him.

Collin turned, sized up the guard, and said, "Collin."

The guard stepped passed him and gestured for him to follow, leading him to the door. He slid the 'NO ADMITTANCE' sign to the left, revealing a buzzer. The guard pushed it, held it a full two seconds, knocked three times for good measure, then slid the sign back. The guard then returned to wherever it was he'd come from, leaving Collin to wait on his own.

But he didn't have to wait long. After twenty seconds there was a buzz, a loud click, and the door popped open. Collin pulled it open, looked into the softly lit room and saw the bars of a cage.

"Close the door behind you," a voice called out from within the concrete.

Enter the cage he did, and he closed the door as requested, all the while a voice, or alarm cautioned him from deep in his gut. He had just placed himself fully at the mercy of someone he didn't know. It wasn't a feeling that he liked. And it didn't help that he could sense someone's presence without seeing them. He felt as though he was being stalked by a wild predator. Whoever it was that he was here to meet deserved his respect, and would demand it, he was sure of at least that much, and of course, that he'd be as respectful as he possibly could.

When the oddly dressed man came into view, stepping into the room's light, and advancing towards the cage, Collin was both relieved and confused. The fear that had just risen within him, and the image of a heartless, square-jawed, scar-faced maniac that had raced through his mind were shattered by the elegant and graceful, if somewhat effeminate man that opened the cage and extended a welcoming hand to shake.

Collin shook the hand, careful not to squeeze too hard, but was immediately on the receiving end of a firm and strong grip. He looked at his host, a handsome and perfectly groomed man who would embody the imagery of a gentleman in the most discerning of imaginations. Collin's eyes met with Hamilton's, and his breath escaped him. Then the man with the amazing eyes turned and asked Collin to join him in the other room, and to please latch the door behind him.

Collin did as he was asked, then made his way into the heart of the parking garage.

"Would you like a drink, beer perhaps?" asked the strange man.

"Please," replied Collin, "thank you."

The dainty man smiled and nodded. He pushed a spot on a wall that had a forest painted on it, and a panel popped open to reveal a hidden fridge. He shook his head, smiled, pushed the panel shut, then took a couple steps and opened another hidden panel, and a second fridge.

"My name is Hamilton, you can call me H. Collin, do you know why you're here?"

Collin thought about it for a second while watching H pull a fancy bottle from his fridge. It looked German from what he could tell. "I really can't say Sir, not specifically...you need me to do something for you, is how I see it."

H smiled, "Glass?" he asked, as he opened the beer.

"That'd be nice," replied Collin.

H retrieved a chilled mug from the freezer and poured the beer while walking towards Collin. He drained the bottle, and handed the mug to Collin so he could grab it's handle. And he wondered at that moment how many people actually drank holding their mug by the handle. He certainly didn't.

"In a way, you're right Collin. You're here because I want something from you. But, I have something to offer as well. Cheers," he said, as he walked back to the wall, and set the empty bottle down on a shelf.

"Have a seat," said Hamilton, gesturing towards a leather recliner that sat across from a larger, much more ornate and plush chair. Collin's visions of blood stained concrete floors in a dank dark room couldn't have been more wrong. The walls were teaming with colour, the floors were a type of Persian rug. Sculptures and instruments, books, maps, it was a lot to take in.

Collin took his seat, "I've walked by this place a hundred times. Never would of thought there was an apartment in here."

"It's not really an apartment Collin. It's my office, and second home, but I don't really exist Collin, neither can my home." said H.

Once more, Collin's eyes were met by Hamilton's, and once more, his breath escaped him. He'd never seen eyes like that. Maybe they were the reason he lived without windows. Maybe his eyes were really sensitive. There was gold in those eyes. Little flecks of gold in bright green orbs. They were eerie, with huge black pupils. It was like looking into the eyes of a cat.

"Right, you don't exist, and I'm not here, got it." said Collin.

"Right. Absolutely right. Are you comfortable?" asked Hamilton.

"Yep, great chair, nice place," replied Collin.

"Perfect. Collin, tell me, how's your Merson treatment coming along?" H asked.

Collin was surprised by the question. That was a name given to the diet he'd incorporated into his life to take control of his health. "Great. I feel great, never better. It's sad more people don't know about it."

"Yes. Absolutely. Informed is not the word I'd choose to describe our nation, or planet for that matter. So many things people ought to know," said Hamilton. "You take care of yourself, obviously. It's admirable Collin, I think you above many appreciate your life. Would you agree with that?" asked Hamilton.

"I can agree with that Hamilton." said Collin, as he thought about the conflicts that had arisen within him because of exactly this question.

"Collin, please, call me H. Now, can I assume that you're ready for a change in lifestyle? Would you miss being a thug?" inquired H.

"Change would be welcome H, Sir. As a matter of fact," Collin continued hesitantly, "I've been working on starting over, you know, got some ideas floating around in the back of my head."

"That's great. Tell me Collin, what happened last night?" asked H.

"I'm not sure what it is you want to know Sir." replied Collin.

"H, please...the target was taken care of, yes, three shots were heard." said H.

"He was alone. Mac took the shot. One in the skull. Then, uhm, he shot the guy's cats." said Collin with a little shrug, "I dunno H."

"Ok. Then you were left to fend for yourself, your driver ditched you. There was mention of an attempted car-jacking, and some messy business with the police." invited H.

"Right. Well, I can't say for sure what happened with the driver. He went around the block, but, he came back, picked us up where he was supposed to." offered Collin.

"Sure," said H, "and when you made your getaway, you somehow attracted a cruiser miles from the scene. What was that about?" H asked.

"Yeah, we were going a little too fast, nearly missed the off-ramp. A cop saw the car swerve." answered Collin.

"Well Collin, I like how you handled the situation. And it's not the first time you've had to think fast on your feet, was it?" pointed out H.

"Uh, no Sir," replied Collin.

"Tell me Collin, are you content with your circle of friends?" asked H, tilting his head to one side.

"Yeah, well. Uhm. H, I don't really have many friends. I know some guys from the gym, we spar, grab a beer once in a while. Then there's Eric and Mac. So, I guess I'd have to say, no." admitted Collin.

"I know Collin, I know...and if there's another thing I know, and I'm sure of, it's that in life, one must choose their friends, not let them choose us. Some things need to be discarded. Often, key moments are all about letting go." H gave Collin a stern but warm look, his eyes were smiling, it seemed. "How's your beer? Can I get you another?"

"No, no thanks, I'm not much of a drinker." stated Collin.

"You're very handsome, do you know that?" asked H.

"Uh," said Collin, unsure of where this conversation was heading, and hoping that it didn't get too uncomfortable, he was after-all, locked in this place.

"I hate hair, you have no idea," said H. "Always have hated it. I don't mean to offend you, but I'd love to be hairless."

"Oh, it has it's benefits, I guess," said Collin, "but, it's always nice to have options, you know, the whole 'no eyebrows' thing seems to wig some people out."

"I think it's beautiful Collin," confessed H.

"Uh, thanks," said Collin.

"I think you'd make a perfect addition to my community. I'm not hitting on you Collin, I like you as a specimen. Smart, strong and attractive can get you far in life, if you understand your advantages." said H with a glint in his eye.

Collin had no comment for this, and so, said nothing.

"Do you live by any credos Collin, do you have a life philosophy?" inquired H.

"Other than eating right, I don't think so," replied Collin.

"I see. Tell me Collin, who runs the world?" asked H.

"Who runs the world?" repeated Collin, "I'm not sure that it's anyone in particular. It's probably more of a 'what' than a 'who'. I'd say it's money that rules the world. Money and debt." answered Collin.

"Ok. But, you don't think anyone controls the money and debt," prodded H.

Collin wasn't sure what to say. He knew that his views were not that of the general public. And he didn't want to offend Hamilton, he thought, 'who knows who this guy was related or connected to?'

"Well, as far as I know, there are a few families who maintain a, cartel I guess, throughout the banking system...private banks, central banks, the Global Monetary Fund...unaccountable and loyal to no one. That's who I think is trying to run the world, but, what do I know?" said Collin.

"Do you trust your government?" asked H.

Collin laughed out loud, and H smiled at the hearty outburst. "No, sorry H. The banks own all the governments, I mean, isn't that what the cold war was all about? Governments securing public trusts for private profiteers? I dunno, that's what I got from the little research I've done."

"Do you have hope for mankind Collin?" asked the odd fella. He was all over the place, Collin couldn't remember the last time he'd been grilled like this.

"Well, as a whole, not really. I mean, there are pockets of people who are trying to change things, but people will always do what they're told to...specially when growing up in 'their' society. We're indoctrinated to be subservient, uh, is my opinion on that." said Collin.

"How would you bring about 'change' Collin? You're smart, let's have it." challenged H.

"Well, I'd get rid of interest. And obviously, I'd have to get rid of the fractional reserve system, and uh, well, countries need to be in control of their money supply, not some private bank. People need to be better educated. And they need to be more involved." Collin said with another shrug.

"So, how would you control the masses, if not through debt?"

asked H.

Collin realized then that H knew a lot more than he was letting on. He was sizing up Collin on more intimate levels than he was prepared for. He thought that this was going to be a business meeting.

"I'm not sure," said Collin, "do the masses need to be controlled? I mean, if money wasn't an issue, and everyone got to do what they wanted with their life, I don't think 'control' would be an issue either. I think people would come together if they weren't raised to compete against each other."

"So, you're an anarchist?" ventured H.

"No, I don't think so...I tend to look to nature Sir. It balances itself, maintains by adapting. I think man could find balance with nature, with itself, if it was allowed to." answered Collin.

"You're not a fan of hierarchy? Not a fan of authority then?" asked H.

"No. Again, looking to nature, we know that we are the same. For some to declare themselves elite, and govern the rights of the many, to limit their existence, under one guise or another...it's ridiculous. No one should profit from infringing on someone else's quality of being. And uh, I think that it's the government's role to uphold that idea...they've bastardized what it really means." said Collin.

"Well said Collin, impressive," smiled H, "but what if it's natural that man cannot have peace? What if it's naturally greedy and violent?"

"Bullocks." said Collin. "I mean, Ok, you could be right, maybe...maybe man's too primitive, emotionally. Maybe jealousy and envy will always rule. But, I think most people are happiest when they're making someone else happy, and if we lived with respect for each other, without lame prejudices, that are man made, not natural, well, if we could live like that, I think people would live to help each other, and be more a part of their communities, you know. We'd have real civility."

"You do have hope." said H.

"You don't?" asked Collin.

H didn't bat an eye. "No." he said flatly. Then he smiled, and followed up with, "your egos will never allow you to see yourselves as equals. But, I really enjoyed your use of the word 'bullocks'. I just don't hear that enough anymore."

Collin thought about what he'd just heard. He feared it to be an accurate observation, but, why did H exclude himself from the statement? It was a little weird.

"You're probably right," admitted Collin.

"I am. It's a sad truth my friend. I'd like to know Collin, the change that you spoke of earlier, the ideas floating around the 'back of your head'. Can I hear them?" asked H, leaning forward in his seat.

"Uh, yeah, I guess so...sure," stammered Collin, who hadn't told anyone of his plans, and was a little hesitant about sharing them. "Well, it kind of has to do with some of the things we've talked about. Narrowing down what life is about and acting on it." said Collin.

"Ok," said H. "Anything concrete?"

"Ya," said Collin. He then reached into his jacket pocket and pulled out his pad of paper. He looked at it, flipping through a few pages. Then he got up and walked it over to H who took it.

"And, what is all this?" H asked.

"Some floor plans, cost estimations and what not. I, uh, I want to build a house, on wheels," said Collin shrugging again.

"You want to, live in a motor-home?" asked H, his eyebrows slowly rising on his forehead.

"Pretty much. I think the best way to go is, buy a trailer, and build the whole thing from the ground up. What I've got in mind would be pretty modern. If you look at the plans, you'll see what I mean," said Collin anxiously.

H took a moment to look at the drawings. They were definitely unique. From the looks of it, one ten by thirty room would serve as every room of a house, one at a time. It was a transformer, where panels opened and swivelled. What was a wall was also the kitchen counter. The same could be said for the tables and benches. Everything was hidden away, and served more than one purpose. Queen size hide away bed, closets, bookshelves...he even had the electrical and plumbing worked out.

"Neat," said H, "so, you'll get yourself a dog, settle in a trailer park?"

Collin chuckled, "Dog yes, trailer park, no. I was thinking I'd travel, lake to lake...ok, maybe trailer park to trailer park. Go north in the summer, head south in the winter, grow my own food...the simple, mortgage free life of a gypsy basically."

"How would you make money? Need fuel to tow a trailer." reminded H.

"Yeah, I'm not sure that I could be independent. Might have to work, get odd jobs to make ends meet, but, I won't really have any expenses." said Collin.

"When were you planning on embarking on this gypsy quest?" inquired H.

"Well, I'm close to having the cash I set out as a goal. Couple more grand and I can buy a used truck, a trailer, the parts and materials, then get to building." beamed Collin.

"You've definitely come to a crossroad haven't you?" said H, sitting in his big chair, tapping his finger tips together rhythmically. His gaze floated up and down, from Collin's head to his feet. "I've made a decision Collin, one that could forever change your life in unimaginable ways. I'll open a door for you, one to another world...another reality. Go home, think about your plans, decide if they can wait. Come back tomorrow, same time, and I'll reveal to you another truth, the greatest truth."

Collin thought about what H was offering, though, he really hadn't any idea of what the offer was. He liked hearing that he could leave. But he felt the nag of not wanting to be included in some scheme because he'd failed to omit himself.

"Mr. Hamilton, Sir, I really am intrigued by your offer, and a part of me wants to come back tomorrow, but another part, the one I've been trying to listen to, well, it just wants to leave all this behind," offered Collin.

"Believe me Collin, you've never known any of 'this'." countered H. "But, I do understand your resistance. A crossroad in life is an exciting happening. All that I ask is another meeting. And Collin, don't worry, you won't be involved in anything without first consenting."

"Right, Ok. Cause, I really don't think I've got it in me anymore. I'm not angry enough to hurt people anymore. Does that make sense?" asked Collin.

"Sure, sure. You don't get angry?" inquired H.

"Not really. Well, to be honest, I do, but it always seems to be the same, uh, issues that piss me off, you know?" replied Collin.

"I see. And, do these 'issues' have names?" prodded H.

"They do. I mean, they're not bad guys. I just can't be responsible for them anymore. I never should have put myself in that situation." said Collin. "I just want to be accountable for myself and my actions. I can never tell what kind of mess I'll wind up in, you know."

"I do," H said with another smile spreading on his lips. "friends, Collin, I believe we already touched on that topic."

"Yeah, don't let them choose you." recalled Collin.

"Well, you won't be working with them anymore, and you won't have to worry about them anymore either." said H

"Yeah," said Collin quietly, "say, uh, H, do you know where they're heading tomorrow? Eric said something about a farm, a new car, and a long drive...didn't sound right to me."

H nodded, he'd expected that Collin would be protective. "Your friends are going to be heading to a farm, true. It's a couple of hours north of here. It's very remote. It's used to grow marijuana and mushrooms mostly. It's a safe-house as well, and, a training facility of sorts. Eric and Max have been tasked with picking up a few pounds of weed from the farm. Simple."

"Ok. Uhm, it's just that, well, I don't really understand why they'd be sent without me. I mean, from a business point of view it may not be wise. They're good guys, don't get me wrong, I just don't..."

"Let me cut you off right there," interrupted H, "I don't think you really believe that. Maybe you do. I'd be more likely to believe that you tell yourself that to reconcile the fact that you've wasted a lot of time, and done some pretty nasty shit with them. Collin, your loyalty is admirable. You owe them nothing, and they would take everything. You know this, and yet, you commit yourself to them."

Collin found what H said pretty well nailed it on the head. He worried about them, wanted to protect them, but wanted nothing to do with them whenever he was with them.

"You can't save them from themselves," said H, again, stating a simple truth.

"No. I know. It's just that, I don't know..."

"They're so pathetic," interjected H.

"Yeah, that might be it," confirmed Collin. "And, I've known them a few years. We got through some pretty rough times together."

"Yes. You were an orphan, isn't that right?" probed H.

"You've done a little research," said Collin.

"I've done a lot of research Mr. Collin McBride," admitted H. "I think that you were dealt a rather shitty hand. And though you're not living high on the horse, or even doing all that well, I think you've got what it takes. I think you're worthy Collin."

"Oh, Ok. Of what?" shrugged Collin.

H clasped his hands together and grinned. His eyes sparkled and widened. He stood from his big plush chair and approached Collin. There was something about H that got Collin's alarm bells a ring dingin'. As he got closer and closer, Collin figured that he must have been forty years old. He looked younger, with his smooth skin and big shiny eyes. He moved like a dancer, or a ghost...so smooth and light. Maybe it was just his weird suit. Collin couldn't tell if there were pant legs or if H was wearing a dress. It kind of looked like a suit from the waist up, only there was no opening. It was sorta like a priest's gown, or cloak, but with an oriental flare. It was very clean looking, very crisp.

Collin couldn't figure out how H got into it. He couldn't see any zippers or buttons. Must just pull it over his head, he decided. And as Collin watched H take his last couple of steps towards him, he followed the folds in H's suit moving like heavy silk drapes. He wondered why he felt so tense. Was he really in any danger here? Collin was pretty sure that he could snap this guy's neck without much effort if he tried anything. But a part of him was a little worried that it just wasn't so. Something about those eyes, his smile, and that handshake made him suspect that H was a wolf in sheep's clothing.

"I can only offer you a choice Collin. You are worthy, in that, you live Collin. You want to live a good, healthy life. You've reflected, you know what's important, and you're putting it into action. You won't settle like most, and one day regret not taking action when you had the chance. That, and you are an attractive specimen, in many ways, right." noted H.

"I'm sorry, you wanted me to leave, I should get out of your hair," said Collin.

"Not at all," replied H. "I was giving you a way out. I've learned from you what I needed. I've made my decision. The rest is up to you. I have all night Collin, you can stay as long as you like, or leave anytime you choose."

Collin wanted to leave. He felt a definite craving for some fresh air, and to be on the other side of that locked steel door. But on the other hand, he felt like he could talk and listen to H for hours. He knew that there was much to learn from the strange man.

"Ok, alright, uhm..." Collin began.

"Tell me Collin," H interrupted, "what's the strangest thing you've ever seen?"

H reclaimed his chair while Collin thought about the question, and about why he was still sitting there.

"I don't know H, damn, I've seen some weird shit. Guys whackin' off in public, skinny women buying their four hundred pound eight year old candy...I see strange things everyday." said Collin.

"Understood. What then, has been the more inexplicable of things you're seen?" H rephrased his question.

Collin thought about it hard. He'd witnessed some bizarre people doing unquestionable things, but he'd always been able to find some reason within them as twisted as they might have been. Collin didn't think that H was after a sick story, he was after something extraordinary."

"You mean, something magical, supernatural?" he asked.

"Sure," said H.

Collin had been sitting squarely in his chair, hands in his lap till now. He recalled a couple of times he'd thought he'd seen things that he wasn't sure of, and slid into his chair a little, lifting his left foot to his right knee. His arms found the chair's rests, he smiled and chucked a little.

"Well, there was this one time...this is going to sound silly, but, I was in the shower, about two years ago. I was just starting to feel the effects of my new diet. Anyways, I was showering, and I pick up this shadow in the corner of my eye. I rinse the soap from my face and look at the shower curtain. Sure as shit, there's someone standing on the other side. I mean, all I can see is a shadow, a shape...but, it's a head, a neck, shoulders, arms, you know, there's someone standing right there."

"Now, I had my own place right, and Eric would pop in

sometimes, so I figured it was him, trying to scare me, or, just seeing what I was doing, who knows right? So, I decide to slide the curtain open and toss a handful of water and soap in his face. I fill my hand, fling the curtain open, toss the water, but there's no one there. I stick my head out of the shower and look around, nothing, no one. I close the curtain, expecting to see a stain, mildew or something in the shape of a person. Nope, clean as a whistle."

"I get out of the shower, grab a towel and check out the rest of the apartment. Nobody. Door's locked, nothing out of place, but, I know that someone was there, I know it...I could feel it, and they left something in the air, a faint scent. Yeah, that was pretty weird. Might not sound like much, but it felt pretty damn real at the time." Collin finished, and drank from his mug.

"Eerie," said H, "any other ghost stories? How's your beer?"

"No, thanks, I'm good," Collin said as he checked his mug and saw that it was still half full, and cold. He took another sip. It was going down well.

"There is one thing H, that I can think of right now, that I see all the time. As often as I see it, it's always strange." offered Collin. "Shoes," he said, "I've seen them all over the place. In parks, ditches, sidewalks, in the bush, washrooms. How does a shoe get misplaced like that? It always looks so sad, you know? So, out of place...unnatural."

"Hmmm," H reflected, "that's a good one. Nothing unusual about abductions, accidents and bullies though. I would imagine that's where they come from, mostly. But I'll give you that it does paint a haunting scene."

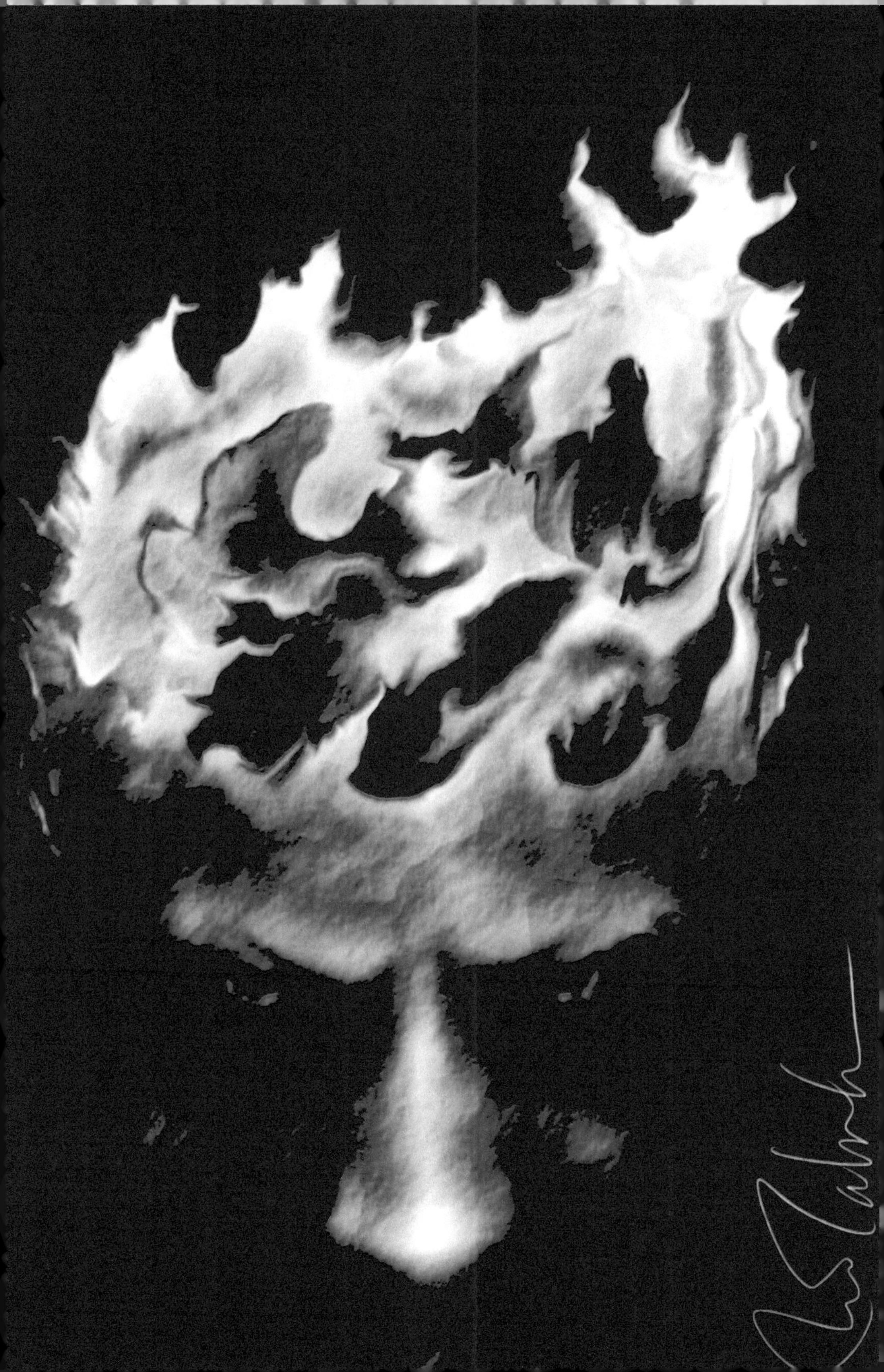

"Yeah, like you said, eerie." added Collin.

"Do you believe in ghosts, ufo's, sasquatch?" smiled H.

"Never seen any of those. At some point though, you have to wonder, I mean, I don't know anything about bigfoot, but, a lot of people have claimed to of seen ufo's. People from all walks of life, including pilots and astronauts, you know? I guess, I know the probability is actually pretty high that there's life in our galaxy, and I'd like to believe it. But, I'd rather know it to be true rather than give in to belief. Guess I'm a little old-fashioned that way."

"If you saw an alien, would you shoot it, or offer your hand?" quizzed H.

Collin took a sip from his mug. He imagined running into a short pot-bellied grey-skinned alien, with a huge wobbly head and big black eyes. Thing was on a spaceship, but it doesn't have any fuckin' clothes on, Collin thought, 'why they always naked and slimy?'

"Alien, man, dog, whatever, always aim to make a friend, but be ready to take aim, right?" said Collin.

"You'd want to know it's nature. What does it want? What can it give me?" said H, philosophically.

"Right," agreed Collin, then he thought about a different kind of alien, a scarier kind of alien. One that was armoured with an unknown technology, and sporting some wickedly sharp looking fangs. "Might want to shoot first," he said, "depends on the alien I suppose."

"Another beer?" asked H as he got up and went to the fridge without waiting for an answer.

"Thanks," said Collin, "why not?"

"Why not indeed," repeated H, as he popped the cap off a beer bottle. He grabbed another chilled mug and brought them over to Collin who gulped down the last of his first, then gave the empty mug to H.

"You know," said Collin, "there was this other time, I was camping years ago. I saw what everyone calls 'ball lightning'. And what they describe and explain it to be is pretty much what I saw. But, the one I saw, well, it was like a ball of electricity, it was blue...and there was a man standing in the centre of it. Like it was a force field or something, and someone was travelling around, flying around in it." Collin shrugged and raised his hairless eyebrows, "I dunno, I only saw it for two, maybe three seconds, then it was gone," he threw his hands up despairingly. "How about you H. What's the strangest thing you've ever seen?"

"Ah, yes...deep, dark and mysterious things indeed. For another time though I'm afraid. What kind of dog were you planning on getting yourself Collin?" H asked with a grin.

"Ha," Collin burst out, "really? Ok, no clue man. One that needs a home and hopefully fetches a ball, you know."

"Were you ever abused Collin, in any of those foster homes that you bounced around from? Any grownups ever take advantage of you?" asked H casually.

Collin should have been used to the line of questioning by

now, but they seemed to come from nowhere.

"Uh, well, yeah. Had some weird shit pulled, but I always fought back. Except one time I guess, well, more than one time really. I was staying with a family, parents, a teenage girl, about fifteen, and a young boy. Parents drank a lot, slept a lot. Anyways, I was like twelve, and the daughter used to come into my room and make me do things. She told me that if I didn't cooperate, she'd tell her parents that I'd raped her, or tried to. Truth is, she didn't have to threaten me at all. I liked it, she was cute. Other than that, got beaten from time to time. Didn't eat all the time either, and it was lonely, but, it was what it was. I got through it, I'm still here right...everyone has a story." said Collin.

"Have you ever molested anyone? Made someone do something against their will for your pleasure?" asked H.

"No. I always felt like I was walking on needles, ya know, didn't take much for me to be expelled, or shipped off to a new foster home as a 'problem' child. I tried to keep my nose clean, tried to be good, so I could find a good home...and, I can't remember ever having urges to, uh, molest anyone." said Collin.

"Tried to be a good boy. But here you sit, a bad, bad man." said H.

"Yeah, well, I rebelled. Against everything and everyone. Anger consumed me H, for a long time. I've done bad things, no doubt, no argument...but I think I'm a good guy, at least, I want to be." said Collin, blushing a little.

"A good bad guy...Sure, I've known a few. How about a game of chess while we chat?" proposed H.

"Chess? Is that what you said? With the King and Queen, that chess?" asked Collin.

"Pawns and Knights, that's right. You don't play," said H glumly.

"No. I mean, never have, that's all." replied Collin.

H smiled, "I'll teach you then."

Over the course of the next few hours, Collin learned how to lose at chess, but he developed a hunger to win. The board game was a great discovery to him. The planning and strategies involved were addictive. Offensive defences, sacrificing, trapping...game after game, question after question, Collin kept playing and answering until nearly three in the morning. He'd had four beer by the night's end when having been up so early that morning and hitting the gym twice that day caught up to him. He came close to capturing H's King a few times, but had to end his lesson without a win.

When Collin left Hamilton's strange hideaway at a quarter to three, he left feeling good about himself. He'd made some fundamental connections that seemed to have gained him an interesting friend and mentor. He'd decided before he left that he would return the following day, and was already looking forward to his next chess match.

The walk home didn't seem to take very long. The cold night air was invigorating, and Collin's mind was wandering, drunkenly. Those were some strong beers. Once in his apartment, he scarfed down some leftover crab salad, brushed his teeth and fell asleep on his couch watching a documentary about aliens. It was a bonus that Eric had made himself scarce, gone to who knows where, doing God knows what. Didn't really matter right now. Collin slept deeply, but his dreams kept him from a peaceful slumber, tossing and turning, mumbling in his sleep all night long. He wouldn't remember much upon awakening, but shadowy figures, glowing eyes and dank musty smells haunted him until morning.

7

Eric and Mac showed up at Hooch's on time, Friday, 7pm. A brand spankin' new black Camaro was parked behind the billiard hall, and the boys couldn't have been more excited about the night's opportunities. Mac was about to knock on the back door to announce their arrival when the door swung open and Hooch stepped out.

"You're on time, good," he said gruffly.

"Yeah man, told ya, we got this," grinned Eric.

"Perfect. Ok. Get in the car," said Hooch as he tossed it's key's to Eric.

"Wicked!" smiled Eric.

"Groovy," said Mac.

They got into the car, fidgeted with the seats and backrests for a minute, then Hooch closed the driver-side door and said, "Ok, see that?" he pointed at a small screen on the console. "That's your GPS. Turn it on...hit that button, good," he said as the screen lit up. When the interactive screen had loaded, he continued, "Ok. There are two locations programmed in there, Home, which is here, and the farm. Touch location, good, see 'Farm'? Touch it, good. Now, just follow that arrow until it tells you that you're there. Got it? You have no reason to stop. Full tank of gas, so just head straight there, they'll be expecting you."

"There gonna be any women there?" inquired Mac.

Hooch leaned over and looked Mac in the eye. "Yep, I imagine there'll be women there. I'd be on my best behaviour if I was you two...show a little respect. Now, you have any questions?"

Eric and Mac checked with each other, everything seemed pretty self-explanatory. "Nope," they said in unison.

"Good. Now, there's a cell phone in the glove box, for emergencies. I don't wanna hear that you fuckin' used it...but it's there, number's are programed...if you need it, which you won't, right?" said Hooch insistently.

"Nope, we're good man," replied Eric.

"Perfect, now get the fuck outta here." said Hooch as he headed back inside the pool hall.

Eric started the car, revved the engine a few times and grinned as the beast's muscles flexed and relaxed, rocking the car gently. He fist-pumped an equally excited Mac, then slapped it in gear and headed for the farm. Eric wasn't used to the kind of power that the Camaro had. The tires squawked, and the rear-end slid out the first time that he touched the gas pedal. It happened again when he turned left onto the street, and he saw people on all sides checking out his sweet ride. One guy gave him the finger, he wasn't sure what that was all about.

They were a block from their departure point when they both saw the sign. Felafel and a milkshake, $4.00. Eric was already hungry and could devour a couple right now. Mac was about to smoke a joint, and he knew that a felafel and vanilla shake would be amazing in about fifteen minutes. So, they made it one block before making their first stop. Eric stayed at the wheel while Mac went in for three orders of chicken felafels and two shakes.

While in the car, sucking on a cigarette butt, Eric got an eerie feeling that someone, or something was watching him. The windows were down, his view unobstructed, but he didn't see anyone paying attention to him. He checked his mirrors, nothing. He even turned down the stereo so that he could listen and potentially hear his stalker. It was the moment that his fingers released the volume knob that he knew the sneak was breathing down his neck. He was about to turn to confront the bastard when a hand grabbed the back of his hair, yanking his head back and down, so that he was held staring at the ceiling. He felt what could have been a blade against his throat. He swallowed hard, and tried to find the courage to say, "take whatever you want man," but his attacker spoke first, whispering, "nice car."

∞

75

Collin must have gotten up from the couch to take a piss at some point during the night, because he'd just awoken in bed to the sound of bells and cheering, a cacophony of ringing and buzzing...sound effects, a game-show, Collin realized, he'd left the tv on.

He didn't feel too good. His head was aching, his neck was tight, and he felt like he was going to shit himself. Collin made himself a coffee and settled in on his throne. He checked his phone, it was half past noon, much later than he'd expected. Half the day was lost to him, and he wasn't sure that he'd make much of the rest of it feeling the way that he did.

It was only a half-hour later, while eating some bacon, two eggs, a tomato and some porridge that Collin started to feel himself again. He'd downed a couple of glasses of water before hopping in the shower, while the bacon was frying, they might have helped too.

Whatever it was that got him un-hung made it possible for Collin to take a walk and checkout another car lot that had some trailers for sale. To his astonishment, he found what he was looking for. A 30ft trailer that was enclosed. It was skeletal inside, which meant that Collin could bring his sketches to life, from scratch, the way that he wanted it. He'd thought about gutting a trailer camper, but his vision would be limited...this was a fresh canvas. And for $3,000, Collin was compelled to inspect every inch of it for flaws or damage.

Finding none, he moved on with his search. When he neared the area where the used trucks were parked, a salesman appeared and greeted him. He was an old man to still be working, Collin thought. Nonetheless, the skinny pot-bellied man with eyebrows like great eagle wings tried to sell Collin something, anything. When Collin pointed at the covered trailer saying "I need something cheap that'll pull that trailer." the old sorcerer looking fella said, "Oh, well then, the bigger the better eh," then tried to herd Collin on down towards the new shiny behemoths.

"No, no, Sir...a pickup, something used, from over there," Collin pointed.

But the old man wouldn't hear of it. He knew that Collin needed power and dependability, and that meant big, new and expensive.

Collin tried to be polite, and succeeded only until he'd reached his limit. He simply turned and walked over to the trucks that he'd come to see.

"Oh, well, ok, guess you know what'cha want eh young fella?" said the old bugger as he trailed after Collin.

In fact, Collin did know what he wanted. A used Ford Lariat, a 250, with leather seats. He'd seen pictures of a white one online that had been well maintained. That was what he wanted.

"Do you have any Ford Lariat's in stock?" he asked the salesman.

"Oh, ya, sure thing, should have exactly what ya need in there somewhere," said the old man, while scanning the lot for bigger fish to fry.

Collin stepped around the side of a big cube van, and started imagining trying to convert it's box into a livable space, when ta-da, just like that, he found what he sought.

It was parked on the other side of the panel truck, and he could only see it's hind quarters, but he could tell from the colours, wheels and tail-light that he'd found his ride. He tried not to smile in front of the old man, but it was an impossible task at this moment.

Collin had barely gotten a peek inside the truck when the salesman asked him if he wanted to take it for a rip, and he wanted nothing more than to test out the truck, but he knew that he'd move on it if he liked the truck's handling, and he wasn't sure that he was ready to commit the cash yet.

Collin mentally bounced the want for it off of the need for it, and checked out the Lariat from it's front end. 'Beautiful,' he thought. The yellow writing on it's windshield said, 2005 Lariat, fully loaded, $11,999!!!. That was more than Collin wanted to pay.

"What's your name?" asked Collin.

"Oh, yeah, sorry...my name's Richard, but everyone calls me Dick," replied the salesman.

"Dick, can you check and see what the bottom line is on this truck for me?" asked Collin.

"Well," Dick huffed, as he furled those wicked eyebrows, "I could probably get'cha $11,500, if the boss is in a good mood."

"Tell you what," said Collin, "you go work on your boss, you tell him I have $13,000 in my pocket for that truck and the trailer I was looking at. I won't go a penny higher." Collin nodded to confirm that he was adamant. He smiled at Dick then walked off, checking his watch to see if it was a good time to hit the gym. It was 3:00pm. "I'll be back later...see if you still want to let me test her out."

"Ya, sure, ok," said Dick as he wandered back towards the dealership, where it looked pretty slow. The boss just might be into making a sale today. The kid would be back, he wouldn't budge, but a sale was a sale, and there was still room for profit on the truck.

Despite his unpleasant morning, the day was shaping up rather well for Collin. He'd pushed himself at the gym, and had a hell of a sparring session, punishing four willing candidates over the course of six rounds.

He'd done a little thinking while he was in the ring. He thought about how he felt when he saw the trailer, and even more, the truck. He'd still be spending a couple grand more than he'd originally budgeted for the combo, but it was still very doable, he'd just have to wait to buy all the material rather than as a whole. Wasn't that big of a deal though, he thought.

He stopped off at his apartment to grab some cash, then stopped for a vegetable medley at a little hippie diner, and made his way back to the car lot while eating his take-out.

He was a good twenty yards from the dealership's front door when a tall husky man in a grey suit pushed through the glass doors. He closed the gap, and was on Collin with only a few long strides. He grabbed Collin's hand and shook while smiling confidently.

"My name's Hal, as in Hal's Motors," he said, jerking his head towards the faded sign above the dealership's facade. "I hear you're looking to make a deal, uh...sorry, I didn't get your name."

"They call me Cash," said Collin.

The big man's smile faded, then reappeared effortlessly, "of course, now, show me what we're looking at here Cash my man."

Collin led Hal to the Lariat, he bumped his fist off of the hood a couple of times, then headed to the trailer.

"Ok, well, that looks like $15,000 to me, wouldn't you agree?" said Hal.

"Not before a test drive," said Collin, as he pulled out his wad of money. "I told Dick 13 grand, and that's what I have for you. We can take that test drive, or we can quit wasting each others' time."

The rest of the negotiation unfolded similarly. Hal spoke of fees and taxes as Collin steered the truck through town. He opened it up and hit the brakes a few times without warning, to test the vehicles integrity, and to knock Hal around a little for amusement.

When they got back to the dealership, Collin drove past the lane where the Lariat had been parked, and instead headed for the trailer. He backed the truck up to it, put it in park, turned it off, then looked at Hal and said, "Thanks for the test drive." He withdrew the wad of cash again, and tossed it over to Hal who caught it, gave it a once over, then slid it into his jacket pocket.

After some paperwork in an uncomfortably quiet dealership, Collin was on his way, pulling his thirty foot trailer out to the storage unit lot with his new Ford Lariat. What a feeling it was, his first vehicle, the one he'd wanted...he made it happen.

The trailer was too high and long to fit in a rental unit, but Collin found a spot beside the farthest building from the road. He was able to hide it behind the unit, between it and a big maple tree. Then he went to one of the units that he used regularly, grabbed some chains and a couple of locks, and secured his new trailer to the tree.

Collin checked his future home a couple of times, made sure that he'd locked the the storage unit, then hopped back into the Lariat and that satisfying feeling of pride in ownership, and of something acquired legitimately. It was his truck, he loved every inch of it, every detail, and it felt good to care for something that strongly, to be so proud.

He put it in drive, checked the clock, 6:05pm, perfect, he could head home, grab some grub, relax a little, maybe go for a drive, then head over to Hamilton's for a few rounds of chess. There was no way Collin was going to lose every time tonight, not tonight.

∞

"Please man, I won't say nothin', take the car man, take it, I don't care...please don't hurt me," pleaded Eric intolerably as the blade pressed against his throat. I'm begging you man, what do you want? What do you want man?" he cried.

"Ahhh, muffin...I'm sorry, did I scare you...did you go peepee?" said Collin through the open window. He dropped the popsicle stick he'd found behind the Camaro from Eric's neck to his lap.

Eric was frozen for two or three seconds before the spazz erupted. "You muth!#*@ &%!#!!!" He screeched for quite a while as he kicked and punched like a spastic piece of spaghetti. "I can't believe you...I coulda killed you bro!" shouted Eric at a very amused Collin.

"Oh, you think that shit is funny, huh? Ha-Ha!" whined Eric as he opened the door and got out of the Camaro to punch Collin in the chest.

This caused Collin to laugh out loud, and Eric punched him again in the chest. And when the laughter didn't stop, Eric threw a fist at Collin's face, hitting him under the nose.

"You little," chirped Collin, as he rubbed his upper lip. He grabbed Eric by the shirt with one hand, and a fistful of jeans with the other, then casually lifted Eric off the ground, and proceeded to shove the little guy through the car's open window, head first.

That was when Mac came out of Naj's, carrying the munchies. He wasn't sure what to make of what was going on, but he was happy to see Collin.

"Hey man, you comin' with us? Want me to grab you a felafel and a shake?" he asked.

Collin shook his head, "Thanks man, but I'm good."

"You're coming to the farm?" inquired Eric, halfway into the Camaro.

Collin let go of Eric, who sat up immediately, pulling his legs through the window, then he practically sprang from the car.

"Wasn't planning on it," Collin shrugged, "but my plans were cancelled...how far is it?"

"Couple hours," answered Eric, fixing his hair.

"Yeah, and there's gonna be chicks there man!" piped up Mac. "I am so getting laid tonight, I can feel it," he said while humping at the air.

"Farm-girls eh, sounds like fun," mused Collin. "So, you're picking up at the farm...where's the drop?"

"We come straight back here dude," said Mac.

"Yeah man, we come straight back, I think," added Eric.

"You think?" echoed Collin.

"Yeah, uh, well, pretty sure...there's only two places in the GPS. Home and the farm. I dunno, they'll tell us at the farm if we're going somewhere else, no?" said Eric.

"Come on dude, it's gonna be a good time," said Mac.

Collin scratched his head and thought about hopping in with the boys, go for a ride in the new car. He took a peek at the backseat, it would be a tight fit. Then he thought about taking his truck. He definitely felt like spending some more time at the wheel.

"Ok," said Collin, "but I'll follow you two in my truck."

"Your truck?" asked Eric and Mac.

Collin smiled and pointed out the Lariat parked across the lot from them, "I thought I'd go for a drive when my plans for tonight fell through. I saw you pulling out of Hooch's, followed you all the way here."

"All the way here, it's only a block," said Mac.

"I was being sarcastic dumbass. Did Hooch tell you not to stop?" asked Collin.

"Felafels man!" said Eric.

"Yeah, right, you're risking your job over felafels. If I'm going with you, we don't stop till we get there, got it?" said Collin.

"What's the big fuckin' deal, relax dude," Max rebutted.

"You're on a job. If shit goes down, you don't want to be ID'd as the guys in this car, right? That means, no stops, no distractions. You're working, be professional, it's that simple guys," protested Collin.

Eric and Mac paused to consider what Collin was trying to teach them. They stared at each other in deep thought.

"Get the fuck outta here...felafels and shakes man, no harm done," stated Eric.

"Yeah, fuck dude...don't come if you're just going to be a buzz-kill...loosen up dude, jeez," said Mac.

"How the hell have you two survived this long?" said Collin, shaking his head and frowning crookedly.

"Whatever dude," said Mac, "can I check out your truck?"

"Yeah, ya, come on," said Collin leading the way to his new Lariat with pride in his heart, and in his step.

Mac set the food and shakes down on the car's hood, then he and Eric met up with Collin by his truck.

"Hop in, check her out," invited Collin.

As always, Mac took the passenger seat while Eric climbed into the driver's.

"Sweet," said Mac.

"Pimpin'," said Eric. "It's a little old, outdated, ya know, but it's clean man, and comfy as fuck."

"It's not old...it's a 2005, only 100k on it, and it's been babied," Collin said, maybe a little defensively.

"No, no...I mean, can't plug in your phone, no navigation or nothin'. It's a fuckin' beauty bro...nice ride Baldy." said Eric.

"Yeah, ok, thanks," said Collin.

"Hey, you wanna christen it?" asked Mac, holding up a joint and admiring it like it was his lover.

Collin shook his head. "No Mac, that's what I'm talking about. You can't show up to business meetings stoned. Gotta have your wits about you," implored Collin, then thought about what he'd just said, and remembered what Hamilton had relayed about people who are beyond help. "Ok," he said, "it's your gig, do whatever you want. I'll follow you, just an observer breaking in my truck. Hey, stop when the farm shows up on the GPS, cool? I'll hang back while you do your thing."

"Sure man," replied Eric.

"You don't wanna christen the truck dude?" asked Mac, unsure of why anyone wouldn't want to.

"Nah, I'm good bud," said Collin, amazed at how little the pair of them had changed in the years that he'd known them.

"Your loss," said Mac, stepping down from the passenger's seat.

"Ok man," said Eric, "try to keep up eh." He left the door open for Collin and gave him a thumbs up.

"Don't drive too fast," said Collin, realizing that he should be a little more subtle with his orders. "You don't want to lose me, I mean, heaven forbid something happens...we gotta be looking out for each other, know what I mean?"

"Sure man...but seriously, keep up. I'm gonna open her up, see what she can do," said Eric, thrusting a thumb over his shoulder at the black Camaro.

"No doubt, I hear ya, just keep me in your rear-view, and stop if you lose me, fair enough?" asked Collin.

"Okaleedoke man...we're movin' on up buddy, look at us eh...it's Friday, we're pimpin', let's rock it brother!" exploded Eric.

Collin hopped into the Lariat and watched his two only friends hurry over to the Camaro. He started the truck and tapped the seek button on the radio. A country station, then another, some chamber music, more country, and so on, until he was right back where he started, with Friday night classic rock. Hotel California was fading out, and Lunatic Fringe crept up from the static as Collin followed the Camaro out of the parking lot. They turned right and made their way north through some heavy traffic. Even when they reached Hwy 21 they couldn't make up any time. Collin didn't have to worry about Eric speeding, but it didn't take long for the duo to start leap-frogging their way to the front, like they were poling for position, and could win the race if they just kept passing cars.

Collin hung back waiting for the traffic to thin, knowing that vehicles would be taking upcoming off-ramps. They were the people who lived in the country and travelled to the city daily for work. They'd all head East or West soon enough. Collin sat back in his leather seat, and watched the black muscle car weave from lane to lane, until he'd lost sight of it. It was a single lane highway, and Eric was passing with every gap in oncoming traffic. He didn't seem to have taken Collin's pep talk to heart, and as usual, it was to hell with keeping a low profile and playing it safe. Collin had to wonder at the kind of mischief that would get them all into trouble this time. Hopefully they'd at least make it to the farm on time, and avoid any scenes until after their business was concluded.

Most of the vehicles travelling north on hwy 21 were now taking side concessions inland as Collin had predicted. Within a few kilometers the traffic thinned dramatically, and Collin was able to open up the Lariat. He was pleasantly surprised by it's power. It was also a very comfortable ride, Collin noted, and smiled to himself in the rear-view as the road opened up before him. His mind wandered , speeding along roads and highways that he had not yet seen, pulling his home from one destination to the next. He thought about the tiles he'd use in the washroom, and about the tint of the wood stain that he wanted. It was at this moment, thinking about his leather recliners, that the day's purchase hit home.

He'd thought about building his home on wheels for a long time. He'd drawn up plans, mostly based on his favourite layouts and schemes from home-shows and online 3D tours. He'd worked out every superficial detail, but it was time to get to work, building it from the ground up. Framing, plumbing and electrical, the fit and finish, the quality would all be on him and his efforts. He knew that he could do it, but he wondered now, how long it would take him to finalize. He'd be doing most of it himself, if not all, and Collin figured he could bring his dream to life within a span of two months. The finishing touches would be the most time consuming, but the trailer would be habitable by that point.

Collin was obviously distracted by his thoughts, because he hadn't noticed driving by the Camaro that had been parked at a rest stop, and was now passing him. Mac's window was down, and he was yelling and motioning for Collin to pull over. The Camaro pulled out in front of the Lariat, then slowed, and pulled off of the road where a lane entered a field.

Collin pulled over behind the knuckleheads, then walked over to the passenger's door and asked what was going on.

"We've been driving for an hour, got another one to go...we're gonna blaze one, you in?" asked Mac.

Collin's instinct was to say no, but, he was off duty, in his own vehicle, enjoying the peaceful drive through the countryside.

"Why not?" responded Collin.

Mac lit a massive joint, took a couple puffs and handed it to Collin, who did the same, and passed it to Eric through the open window. They continued with the rotation while listening to a song about a highway to hell. Mac played an air guitar, Eric rocked out on an invisible drum set, and Collin leaned against the car's hood taking in the reddening sky, wanting to follow the sun that was about to slip under the horizon.

"How's the car handle?" asked Collin as a great plume of thick smoke flowed from his lips and nose.

"Like a fuckin' dream man!" praised Eric between tokes.

Mac looked up at Collin who was still standing by his

window, he cocked an eyebrow, "it's fast dude, real fast."

"No doubt," said Collin.

"Faster than that truck of yours, that's for sure," added Mac.

"Agreed," said Collin.

"What, you think you could take us?" asked Mac, picking up on something in Collin's voice that wasn't there.

"Nope, that's alright," said Collin patiently.

"Yeah, cause we'd blow your fuckin' doors off guy." laughed Mac.

"Ok, thanks for the doobie, keep the rubber side down boys," said Collin as he returned to the Ford.

Collin didn't wait for the Camaro to merge. He pulled out onto the highway and continued on his leisurely way, knowing that the boys would soon catch up and pass him on their way to victory in the one vehicle race they were fated to win.

The next hour rolled on without incident. The music he'd been listening to wasn't matching his mood, and he found himself scanning the radio stations again for something suitable. A melody came on that made his flesh break out in goosebumps, and he listened to it, knowing that it was classical music, and loving it regardless. When it was over, a woman's voice said something along the lines of 'that was Mozart's tenth symphony, Gran Partita,'...and Collin made a mental note to give Mozart a good listen sometime.

Collin saw the duo when they passed him after smoking the

joint, and then again an hour later, parked on the side of the road where it was lined with tall pines.

"About time, been waiting ten minutes dude," said Mac when Collin joined them.

"Ok, what's up, the farm close?" asked Collin.

"Uhm, well, the GPS says to take a left right here," said Eric, pointing across the road at a narrow slit in the dense pine forest.

"Ok, how far are we from it?" asked Collin.

"Well, it says 3.5km. Kinda weird, no? Isn't that all lake out there?" asked Eric.

"Yep. A few kilometers out. The farm must be on the water. You sure this is right?" asked Collin as he peered down the tall sliver of a clearing that sank deep into the woods. They were tall trees, bare for twenty feet from the dirt up to their thick canopies, which rose fifty feet up. There was still a hint of the sun's dying light above the trees, but a thick darkness lay beneath them.

"That's a narrow lane," commented Collin, "can't really turn around once you head in."

"This is the spot man, look," said Eric, pointing to the GPS screen, "3.5km to go."

"Yeah," reflected Collin, "might not be a good idea for me to follow you in there."

"We got this guy, no worries eh," said Eric.

"It's our show," stated Mac, "they might be pissed if we show up with some dude."

"Yeah, I can't really argue with that," said Collin, his face contorted in deep thought, exhaling a long breath loudly through his nostrils. He bent down, placed his hands on the car's roof, and looked in on his pals. "You're good to go, are ya?"

Eric and Mac nodded and gave a thumbs up in unison.

"Alright," said Collin, "guess I'll wait tight, maybe go for a little drive. Gimme a shout when you're leaving, or, if anything goes wrong, cool?"

"Yeah man, and if they're cool, I'll ask if you can come..."

"No," interrupted Collin, "don't do that Eric. Just do what you came here to do, get what you came to get, right, then we can get back on the road. Don't mention me, they might get nervous...never know."

"Ya, ok man. No promises though, gonna be a buncha hot bush bitches there man," grinned Eric, "we might stay the night."

"Do you hear the words that come out of your mouth?" asked Collin.

"What?" replied Eric, grinning.

"Just watch out for their 'bush boyfriends' there bud," Collin chuckled, imagining Eric and Mac hitting on every female they'd see, knowing how pitiful their attempts could be, and how they'd mastered rejection like it was a badge of honour. "Be yourselves, but be gracious, be polite, and you'll do just fine...and probably get more jobs like this, this is gravy right here...am I right?"

Mac pounded his fists on the dashboard, "Let's go man! I'm fuckin' jonesin' here."

"Holy fuck dude, relax...chill man," said Eric. "Yeah, we better get going big guy, gonna be late."

Collin checked his watch, 8:53pm. The sun was almost gone. It was all but a golden hue splitting the dark horizon from the red sky, which was getting darker by the minute.

"Ok, I'll see ya in a bit," said Collin, standing up and rapping his fist on the hood for luck.

"I'm stopping for pancakes on the way back...just sayin," grinned Eric.

"Of course, whatever you want...I'm getting the munchies too, pancakes sound good." said Collin. "Give me a shout, eh."

"Later brother," said Eric. He then checked his mirrors for traffic and set off for the farm. The Camaro crossed the highway, it's headlight's piercing the darkness and showing the path that it would now take.

Collin stood on the side of the road watching the taillight's move further into the treeline. After a minute, he could still see them. Small red dots, glowing like eyes in a sea of black, under a crimson sky. He was trying to gauge the distance that the car had travelled when the red lights disappeared. It looked like they'd drifted to the right, then they were gone, and Collin sighed as a weight was lifted from his chest. He looked up and smiled at the amazing sky.

He was thinking about possible destinations that he could hit from here that wouldn't take him too far out. There was a nice little town on the water a half hour north, he'd been there once years ago, and was told by a local fella that the town had once been taken over by a biker gang, and that the army was brought in to clear them out.

It was the closest destination, and Collin wasn't sure that he wanted to stray that far. He reached for his phone in his pocket so he could check out a map, and was spooked by a sound. A snapping twig in the woods across the road. He strained his eyes, looking for movement, and saw nothing but darkness. Collin stood there a good minute, watching and listening, but nothing caught his attention.

He climbed back up into the Lariat and checked his phone's map from the comfort of his leather seat. He was right, there was nothing for a half hour in any direction. Biker town to the north, hick-town to the east, and provincial park to the south. Other than staying put, those were his options. He decided to drive down the road until he found a view of the lake.

He was about to reach for the ignition when Collin heard what sounded like a grunt, followed by a snort. It sounded like a bear, but as far as he knew, there weren't any bears in this part of the province. He heard another snort, then a low rumbling growl.

Collin looked out the open window trying to identify what

was making all the noise, and like a dog's warning, the growl continued from the trees. He scanned the woods from side to side, up and down, but saw nothing, it was too dark. He checked his rear-view mirror, then the road ahead of him. He thought about starting up the truck, cranking the wheel to the right, and backing up, so that he could illuminate the woods, and the animal, but this time, when his hand went to the ignition, his phone rang, and he jumped in his seat.

"Hello," he answered.

"You damned fool!" yelled a disgruntled Hooch.

"Excuse me?" replied Collin.

"I just spoke with Mac...I wanted to make sure they'd made it, and he tells me you tagged along," said Hooch in a huff.

"Hi Matthew, yeah, sorry, I bought a truck today, just getting to know it...hmmm..I uh, I've got something stalking me Hooch...I can see it's eyes..." Collin trailed off.

"Where are you, exactly?" asked Hooch.

"Just on the side of the highway, across from the entrance to the farm," answered Collin.

"Get the fuck outta there!" barked Hooch.

"What? Why...what's up? I'm in my truck, no worries," said Collin.

"Collin, please, get away from there, for Pete's sake man, you're in danger!" implored Hooch.

"The fuck you say, I'm in danger? What about the boys?" asked Collin.

"Damn...just forget about 'em Collin...get your ass in gear, now!" commanded Hooch.

"You tellin' me they're in danger? What the hell's going on?" demanded Collin.

"Get back here, and I'll tell you everything I know kid. Leave right now, head straight here, just go Collin, go!" squealed Hooch.

"Ok, ok, calm down. I can't just leave them here Matthew, not if I can help them," Collin pointed out.

"Christ! There's nothing you can do Collin, believe me, I'm sorry. Now think about yourself, get your ass clear of the farm, pronto buddy," said Hooch in a rush.

Collin's eyes hadn't left those of the animal that was watching him. They were big, like a wolf's, or a cougar. There was a greenish glint reflecting in them. "You know what this animal is that I'm staring at?"

There was a long pause, a deadly silence, if not for the throaty growl that still drifted across the highway. "Hey, you there?" asked Collin.

"Yeah, ya. I might know what it is. Trust me, you don't want to meet it. Again Collin, I'm begging ya, scram man, it's time to flee...I'll tell you all about it later, promise," urged Hooch.

"I might take you up on that, a little later though. I'm gonna stick it out here," said Collin.

"Ok man, listen, Eric and Mac are gone, ok. Being 'sent' to the farm is basically a death sentence, alright, that's why you weren't on this one. They outlived their usefulness, and they're fuckin' liabilities Collin. Just taking care of business, in-house, understand?" said Hooch.

"What the...I can't believe what I'm hearing. You sent them to their deaths? I'm sitting here while they're walking into a trap?" burst Collin.

"Collin, whatever you do, don't go after them. I repeat, do not go after them. Just get outta there...it's too late, there's nothing that can be done," pleaded Hooch.

"Bullocks," said Collin, "we're gonna have a little chat about this when I get back Hooch."

"Wasn't my call man! You're not supposed to be there for a reason...now don't be there, capiche!" said Hooch.

"Bye for now, I'll see ya when I get back," said Collin, then hung up the phone while Hooch apologized and pleaded some more.

Collin dialed Eric's phone, then Mac's, but no one answered. He looked out into the woods for the green eyes, but he couldn't locate them. He lifted his centre console, and pulled out his .44, it's holster and the Tai-pan. He slid the blade into it's harness, which he was wearing on his back, then strapped on his shoulder holster. He checked the gun's clip, it was full, and there was one in the chamber. He flicked off the safety and slid the gun into it's leather home. He took a deep breath, reached for the keys in the ignition and twisted. The truck roared to life, then Collin heard a deep howl rise in pitch ever so slowly, and hang on a single note until it finally faded. He rolled up the window, locked the doors and ventured into the woods.

∞

8

Hooch sat nervously behind his desk, swirling some scotch around in his glass. He huffed, and puffed, then downed his drink in a single gulp. He spun in his chair and stared at the white phone for a moment before grabbing it's receiver. There was no number to dial, and the phone had no dial, but when Hooch lifted it to his ear, a phone was ringing at the other end. Hooch got nervous, the phone rang again. Each tone seeming to linger for an eternity, but the silence between them felt even longer. It rang again, and Hooch contemplated hanging up. It rang again, and he was counting the seconds, anticipating the silence, when someone answered.

"Good morning," said a voice at the other end.

"Oh, good morning," replied Hooch, checking the clock on his wall. It was after 9pm. "Uhm, it's Matthew, sir, well, it's Hooch."

"Yes...what can I do for you," replied the calm voice.

"Well, uh, I'm not sure it's anything, but I thought you should know...I just spoke with Collin, and, uh, he was parked at the entrance to the farm. He took his new truck for a drive, followed the two that you..."

"How long ago did you speak with him?" interrupted the voice.

"Just now...I just hung up," replied Hooch.

"Thank you Matthew, have a good night," said the voice before the line went dead.

Hooch looked at the receiver for along moment while he wondered if he'd see Collin again...if he'd have to explain things to him. He hoped to see him again, but the thought of answering to an angry Collin made his blood run cold.

Hooch thought about the first time he'd met Collin. It was right out front, in his billiard room. He'd started showing up in his mid-twenties to play snooker. He was working for a landscaper or construction company and would come in at the end of his day for dinner and a match against anyone who would care to play. He'd always offer to pay, and usually lost, although he was a decent shot. It took him a few months to start winning consistently, and by then had become a regular fixture at the pool hall.

Eric and Mac had also been regulars, but they stuck to the video games in the arcade section. Hooch had his eye on them when they were teenagers. He'd given them a taste of a few select narcotics then sent them out to sell for him. It didn't last long, as the nitwits wound up using as much as they sold and always came back short-handed. They worked off their debts by hitting the pawn shops and jewellery stores that Hooch instructed them to.

They had managed to stay out of each others way for a long time, but one night, Eric and Mac were up for a fight, and they zeroed in on Collin. Mac had pulled a knife, and when he attacked, missing his mark, he was met with a wind-killing uppercut to his gut that caused him to barf. Hooch had broken it up before anyone could get seriously injured, and for whatever reason, from then on, the three of them were always seen together.

Collin didn't realize that the billiard rooms were also a part of a criminal hub. And that on any given day you could find contract killers, arsonists, hustlers and pimps knocking back drinks and playing poker. Briefcases, suitcases and bowling ball bags came and went carrying cash and weapons like clockwork.

Hooch's operations had a few rough years, where the police watched his place of business like hawks. He was certain that it had been bugged too. When everything seemed to be at it's worst, when all was lost, and he knew that he'd wind up in prison, or worse, two cops had shown up carrying that bloody white phone. They'd promised him no further police interference, as long as he agreed to do whatever the white phone told him to. It wasn't much of a choice, and even though a weekly payment was soon being requested by the same two cops, Hooch soon found himself in a position where he was able to pay their racket premiums. And as promised, the police left him, his business and his employees alone. In fact, the boys in blue had earned their payments by cleaning up a few messy situations for him.

Over the years, Hooch had developed a liking for Collin. He'd felt bad when he brought Collin into the business, but the kid needed a leg up, and it was the only way that Hooch knew how to help him. Eric and Mac were both psychotic, or damn near to it, and Hooch had figured that Collin could level out their depravity, he'd act as a leash for the dogs.

As it turned out, Collin had been a pretty angry young man, and he didn't shy from his share of high pressured negotiations. He'd even killed on a number occasions. Collin had shot a dozen at least, drowned a few others, and just last year, killed three with his bare hands, accidentally.

The first guy had stolen from one of Hooch's gambling rooms. A poker dealer who tried to sneak off with the house's roll during his break . The punk hadn't gotten far before the police caught up to him and delivered him to Hooch. It was during Collin's interrogation of the thief, during which he wouldn't stop crying and snivelling that Collin had slapped him across the throat.

Collin had only meant to shut him up by backhanding him lightly, but he connected squarely with the guy's Adam's apple. He'd choked and gasped for air for a full minute before convulsing to his death. Collin had been lucky that the cash had been recovered, and that the degenerate wasn't missed.The second and third had been killed by single blows as well. One had taken a right hook to the head that broke his neck and put him down instantly. The other had received a straight left to the chest, which broke ribs, and punctured a lung. A blow that might have been survivable had the man's heart not been stopped by it.

Collin's might and ferocity was soon well known, respected

and feared. The man who dodged harm, and killed with a single punch. He wasn't the shy, timid pushover that Hooch had feared him to be, but he was able to manage the dumb-dumbs, and make a living doing it.

On the other hand, it was a point of regret for Hooch. He'd created a weapon in Collin, and gave his anger a purpose. A softhearted, well meaning and mannered young man whose entire life seemed to be a shame, coming into his own as a goon. When he changed his diet and took up boxing, he was transformed. Collin had doubled his mass, and was as dense as mahogany. Hooch was certain that with a little tactical training, Collin could easily be one of the most lethal men he'd ever heard of. Word on the street was that sponsors had been approaching the gym where Collin worked out. They wanted to set up fights for him, and were promising him huge payouts, but for some reason, Collin wasn't interested in a boxing career. It was just a great way of keeping in shape as far as he was concerned.

Hooch imagined that Collin could have been just about anything, but opportunities had been few and far in between for him. A decent man, stumbling down the path of indecency. Finding his way to the top of the bottom, distinguishing himself from the rest of the trash. Hooch had watched the young man take control of his life, redefining himself physically and mentally, trusting in his own intelligence and abilities. Hooch hadn't been surprised when only a month ago, Collin had informed him of his desire to quit, and asked for his blessings. Hooch had been more than happy to tell Collin that he was free to come and go as he pleased, and that he owed no one anything.

"Damned phone," said Hooch, knowing that Collin's hand had been forced again, and when he was so close to making a clean getaway. "Sorry buddy," he said, also knowing that what Collin would face tonight, if he chose to storm the farm, would be the end of him. As tough and as fierce as he was, Collin would be shredded to a pulp, and his blood would feed the ground, like so many of the farm's victims before him. There were far worse things out there than pimps and killers.

"Bloody phone."

∞

Collin crossed the highway and and pulled up to the treeline. He flicked his high beams on and looked at the path that cut through it. Orion, the instrumental song was starting to pick up, getting heavier over the radio. Collin cranked it up to drown out the sounds of howling and growling, snorting and sneezing that were all around him now. He gripped the Lariat's wheel and hammered the gas. The truck lurched forward and was immediately hit by something big on the passenger's side. Collin didn't take his eyes off of the trail, or his foot off of the gas. As he gained speed, the truck was bombarded by thuds and bangs, and they came from every angle. He could see blurs of movement, but it was like trying to spot shadows in the dark. Things were either being thrown at him, or they were charging and ramming him. He was being rocked, but the truck was steady and powered through the onslaught.

He was trying to block out the sound of his new truck's body being scraped and gouged. It sounded like knives were making their marks along the truck's sides, and he was pretty sure that he was dragging something...that he was pulling an animal that was clinging to his truck. He noticed the upcoming corner just as something heavy struck the front of the truck, then spiralled over the cab and landed in the truck's box. Collin was almost certain that it was the torso and front legs of a deer.

The Ford handled the right turn like it was on rails. It was a long slow turn that seemed to go on forever. Collin was starting to wonder if he was going to wind up back on the highway when the path curved left. He steered into the corner, when something else slammed into the truck, smashing the passenger's side of the windshield. It too landed in the back of the truck, and when Collin checked his rear-view he saw the big red eyes, lit by the light on the back of the cab...they were staring at him through the sliding window that separated them.

He slammed on the brakes, and whatever it was cracked it's head on the top of the cab, smashing the break light. The owner of the eyes roared and Collin pushed the gas pedal to the floor. The beast stumbled backwards, but didn't fall out of the box, so Collin hit the brakes again , and the animal was flung forwards, towards the cab again, but this time, it managed to leap from the truck, over the cab, and landed on the path in front of Collin.

"Hooo-leeee shit!" said Collin, then stepped on the gas, managing to run down his aggressor and clip it's hind quarters as it tried to get up and out of the way.

The path was still drifting left, and Collin tried not to think about anything other than keeping the Lariat aimed down the centre of it. It was very smooth, and the truck liked it, but the constant barrage from things trying to derail it was hindering his ability to keep a true line.

When he realized that a right turn was up ahead, three powerful thuds rocked the truck one after another. Both wheels on the left side came off the ground, and Collin jerked the wheel to the right, sitting the tires back down on the dirt. No sooner had he recovered, three more jolts hit the Ford from the right. There wasn't much that Collin could do but hang onto the steering wheel while the truck rolled onto it's side. He was sliding into the trees at 70km/h, and narrowly missed being decapitated by a tree that took the entire top of the cab off, leaving Collin clutching to the passenger's seat, debating whether he should jump from his brand new wreck.

He prepared himself for a forceful lunge, and waited for a tree to go whizzing by, then dove into the woods, knowing that the trees were spaced a few meters apart, and hoping that he'd avoid hitting one. He hit the ground hard, but stayed loose, and rolled through the soft mossy pine needle riddled undergrowth like a rag-doll, until finally, he was stopped by a tree trunk. He'd been falling backwards, and struck the pine while upside down, his legs and crotch taking the brunt of the blow.

He hadn't the time to assess whether anything was broken when something grabbed his leg and lifted him off the ground. Five sharp claws sank into his chest, and Collin felt them grip him, and take his entire weight while he was rotated in the air until he was right side up, being held off the ground by claws that pierced his ribcage. He was face to face with a werewolf, and found himself wondering why he didn't listen to Hooch, and why he always seemed to do things the hard way.

He wrapped his left arm around the beast's forearm while his right hand went to the small of his back. The wolf-man roared, and Collin swiped at it's throat with his trusted Tai-pan blade.

The monster dropped Collin and it's hands flew up to the wound. Blood jetted out from between it's fingers in pulsing plumes, soaking Collin in a warm greasy layer. He pulled his . 44 from it's holster, aimed at the kneeling beast's forehead, and fired a round between it's eyes. The werewolf's head snapped

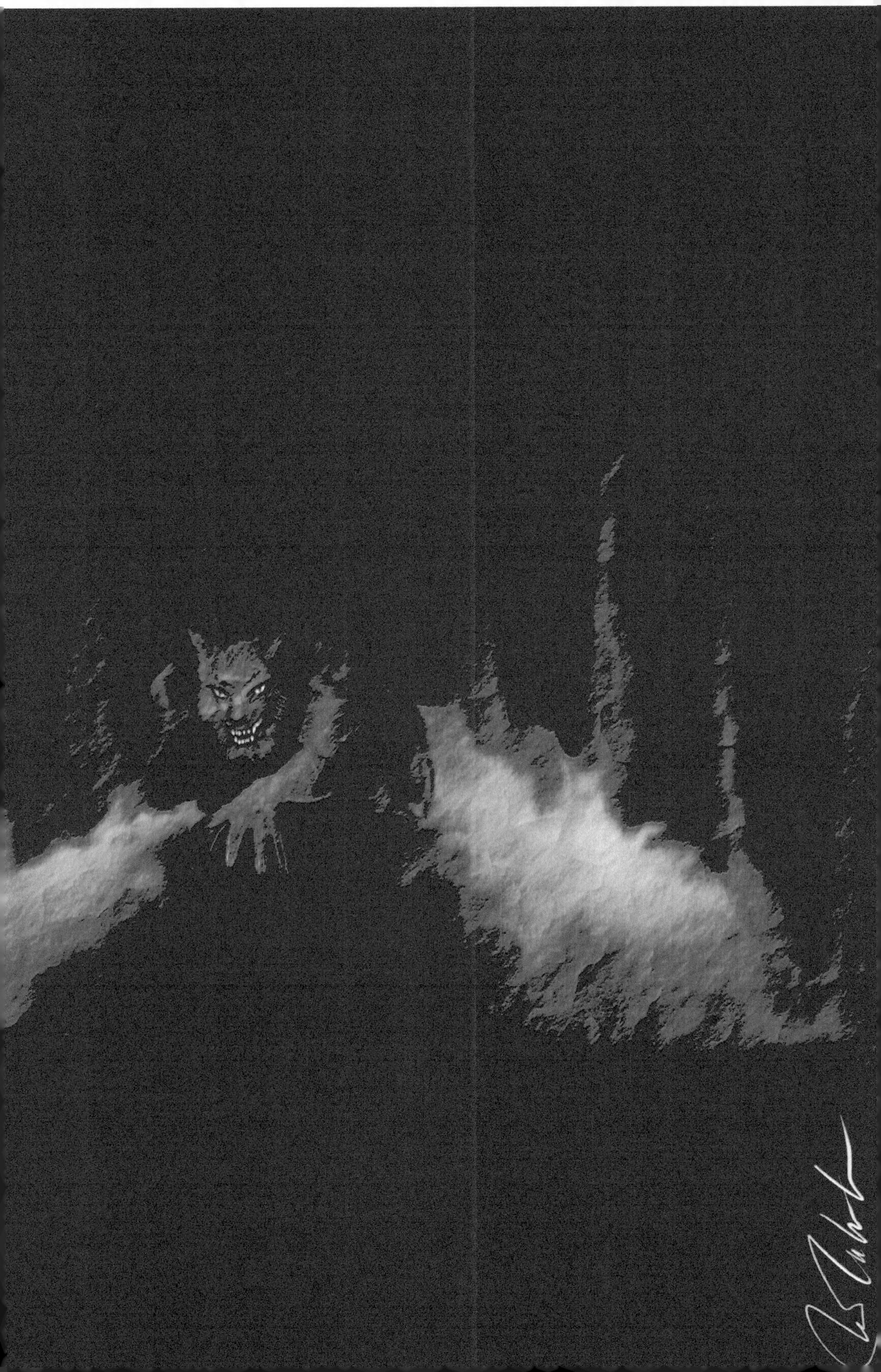

back, then slumped forward as it's body went limp and fell to the dirt, it's face breaking the fall with a thump.

That was one, of how many, there was no way of knowing. Collin listened as the remaining hoard howled at the falling of their brother. He gathered himself and tried to get his bearings. The truck was to his right, the lights were still on, the road was to his left, so, the farm must be somewhere behind him.

Collin holstered his pistol, then bolted for what he hoped was West, armed only with his deadly dagger in his left hand. He managed a few strides before knowing without a doubt that the chase was on. Barking erupted, deep, guttural sounds that Collin felt in his bones, like a nauseating bass line. He ran without being able to see where to.

He heard a monster crashing towards him from his left, and pushed off with right leg as hard as he could, launching himself towards his attacker. He led with his shoulder, his head tucked, his legs curled up under him, and his hand on the butt of his gun. When they collided in the air, Collin pumped four quick rounds into the werewolf's abdomen before it landed on top of him, rolled off, then thrashed around, clawing at it's stomach.

Collin got to his feet quickly, and again tried to determine which way to run, when a face so white it seemed to glow in the darkness appeared only a few feet from him. The face smiled, showing off it's fangs, then it opened it's mouth wide, and shrieked a war cry as it sprang towards Collin, arms and claws outstretched. Collin took a step back, grounding himself, he put his right hand on the butt of his knife, and with both hands, thrust the blade forward. The ghoulish creature groaned when Collin's Tai-pan plunged hilt deep into it's cheek, then it gasped when two rounds tore through it's chest. Collin pulled down on the blade's handle, and struck upwards with his knee, crushing the other side of the creatures face. He twisted the knife, then pulled it out as his attacker fell to it's side, screaming in pain.

Again, Collin tried to get a sense of where West could be. He heard a growl, it was above him, then he saw what he was looking for. He saw red, the last of the sun's dying light, to his right. He was almost through the forest, he could see where the canopy of darkness ended. He dashed towards the promise of open sky, while a werewolf crashed from tree to tree in pursuit. Others were nearby as well, but Collin was getting the sense that this was a hunt, and that they would attack one at a time...at least, he hoped that it was the case.

He heard his pursuer land in and jump from a tree, then he dove to his left when he realized that he didn't hear the wolf landing in another one, and as he'd suspected, there was a mighty crash to his right where the monster practically belly-flopped it's landing. It growled and looked at Collin who was hunched on one knee, drawing his pistol. Collin saw the beast's eyes, and put a bullet in each one, then put the gun back into it's harness, and sprinted once more towards the opening.

His heart was racing, and Collin tried to slow it as he ran, by breathing deeply. His chest was sore, but a little numb, thankfully. Other than that, he felt great. He'd surely run out of ammo before he got tired of fighting for his life. He checked his jacket, he had two more clips. He'd counted his shots, and if he was right, he had three left...two in the clip. He swapped it for a fresh one mid-sprint.

He wasn't sure why they weren't attacking as he made his

mad dash for the clearing, but Collin took advantage of every step, like he was running for his life, one could say.

With twenty yards left between him and his immediate goal, Collin had to ponder what it was that he was running to blindly. Maybe he was being herded the whole time. Maybe the trap was up ahead. He slowed his stride, and stopped at the edge of a field. It was a relief to see the sky again, even-though it had grown very dark. Collin could still see in the moonlight, and noticed to his right the road that he'd been trying to stay on. He walked quickly in it's direction while listening intently for any sign of his tormentors.

He reached the road, and was again awash in a feeling of relief and hope, but it was short-lived, for on either side of him, blocking the road, were a dozen ghouls and werewolves.

Behind him lay the woods and some monsters. Ahead was the farm and some monsters. On either side, was quite possibly his only hope. Row upon row of marijuana plants, seven, eight feet tall in places. They were dense, and stank something fierce. The sweet, pungent aroma was thick, and Collin kept wondering if he'd be able to wash the sticky scent off, and how many showers it would take, if he ever got to have another one.

He was debating his options, going left, running into the weed field and shooting anything that moved...going right, with pretty well the same game plan, or standing his ground, and taking down each of his opponents as they approached.

The monsters must have sensed his intentions, and began to advance on him, keeping a solid formation. Some of the werewolves were on all fours, while others were walking tall, but all of their jaws were snapping as they sniffed and licked at the air.

The ghouls were hideous. Skinny pale wisps of loathsome things dressed in rags. They were gaunt, and looked too weak to stand. Their skin was too tight, and it pulled at their mouth and eyes.

It was a huge wolf that charged him first, when Collin saw lights in the distance, and kept his eyes on them for a second too long, a beast ran him down from behind. It wasn't making any noise other than it's footsteps, but Collin heard them. He pulled his gun and aimed for it's face.

"ENOUGH!"

The beast stopped in it's tracks, looking up, Collin looked at the rest of them, none were moving. He looked up to where the voice had come from. He saw nothing, and careened his neck, trying to see every which way in the dark star filled night.

"Collin," said the voice.

Collin pivoted on his feet, and spun the gun around.

"Please," said H, "I really don't like having firearms pointed at me."

Collin hesitated, then lowered the pistol, keeping it aimed at the dirt near Hamilton's feet.

"I'd say that I got here just in time, wouldn't you agree?" asked H.

"Where'd you come from?" asked Collin, still shifting his eyes from creature, to monster, to H.

"I was in my office, and your friend Matthew contacted me...told me what you'd gotten yourself into...I'm sorry I had to cancel our evening Collin...had that not happened, this would not be happening now."

One of the werewolves stepped from it's line, and regressed back into it's human form while walking towards Hamilton. When it reached him, it stood naked beside him, and said, "asshole cut Daphne's throat, then shot her in the face. Got Hank in the gut too, he's hurtin'. One of your guys got fucked up pretty good, and uh, Jake got both his eyes shot out...fuckin' brutal."

Hamilton listened to the naked man, shaking his head in astonishment. "I'm sorry Buck," he said, "but they'll be fine...Daphne's such a pretty girl. I hope that there's no scarring. Buck, you were trying to kill him, were you not? Of course he's going to fight back, look at him, what did you expect?"

"I expected him to do what everyone does, you know, scream, faint, piss himself," answered Buck.

"Not this one Buck," said Hamilton, approaching Collin, "what do you have to say for yourself?"

"Well," said Collin, "have you boys found the light, and let the love of Jesus Christ our lord and saviour into your hearts?"

Two of the werewolves laughed like hyenas until Buck gave them each a glare.

"You can understand that Buck here is upset, can't you?

Collin, you shot his wife in the face." said H.

"She wasn't playing nice," said Collin.

"I'm gonna feed you to my kids!" yelled Buck, kicking some gravel at Collin.

"Now now," said H, "we're all friends here, believe it or not."

"Tell that to my truck," said Collin.

"Was your vehicle damaged?" inquired H.

"It's in pieces," replied Collin.

"I'm sure that we can work something out," said H, "now, how about we make our way down to the house."

Collin was about to ask where Eric and Mac were, when something struck him from behind, in the head. The last thing he heard before everything went black was H asking, "now, what did you go and do that for?"

∞

9

Collin came to slowly, like a man crawling out of quicksand. He wanted to open his eyes and rub his neck, but there was a conversation going on, and he decided to eavesdrop. He was laying on his side, on what felt like a couch. There was a pillow propping up his head, which was pounding, especially around his eyes, and his temples were throbbing.

He recognized Hamilton's voice, who was telling someone that he wasn't too happy with the new strains of weed that they'd grown in one of their greenhouses. A woman had agreed. She didn't like the taste, and the high wasn't strong enough. She asked Hamilton if he'd tried the 'Blue Bomber' that someone named Lisa had grown. He had, and rated it a ten. He said that he'd gone out after smoking some, and that he'd come back to his office drenched with unfallen rain, as he'd been soaking up cloud mist while soaring around aimlessly in the night.

Collin listened, amazed by what he was hearing and feeling. Monsters were talking about getting high, that's what he was hearing. What he felt was the the butt of his gun against his ribs, and the Tai-pan still gripped in his left hand.

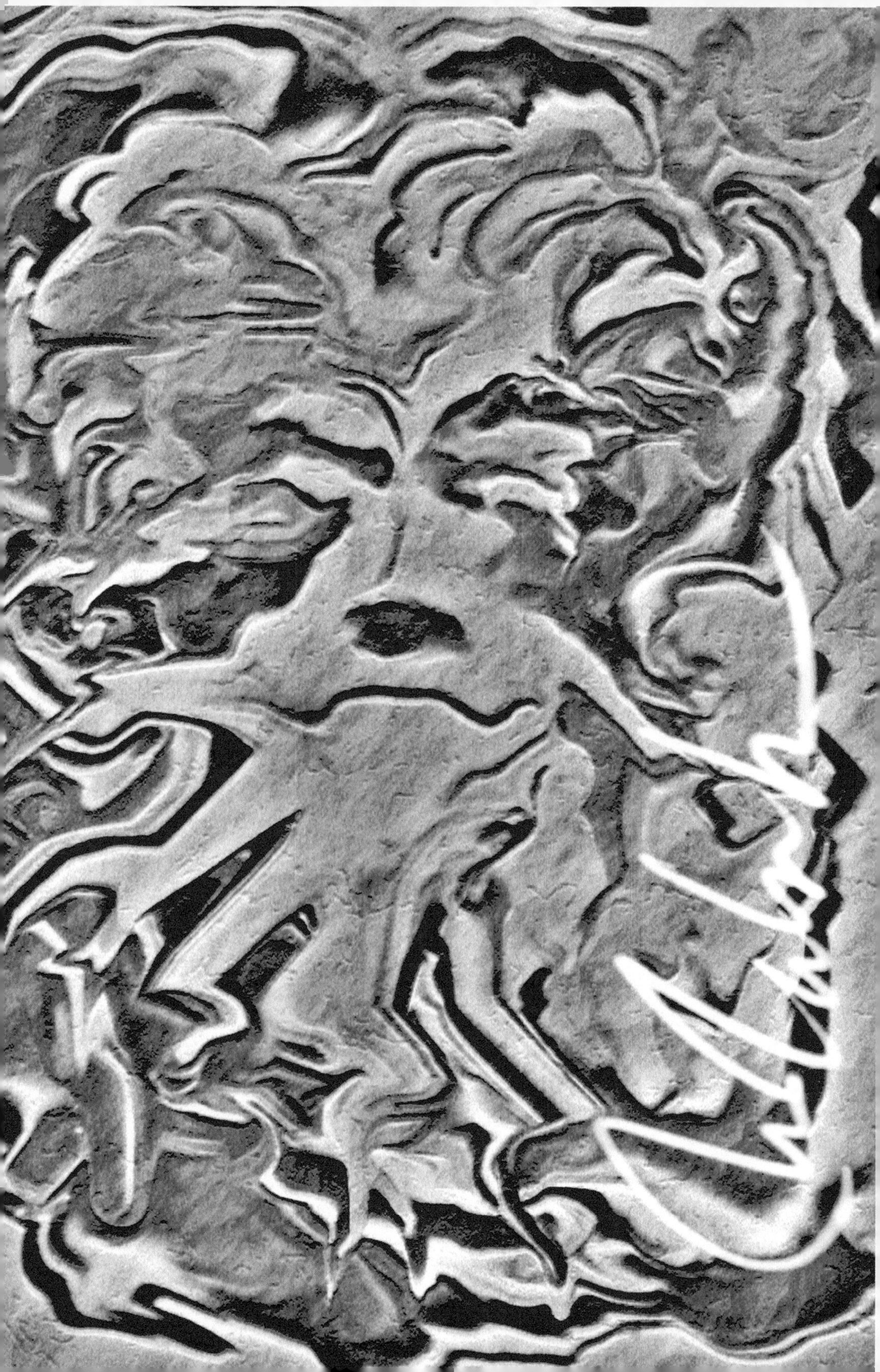

The conversation then turned towards someone named Anon who was seemingly going to be missed, by H in particular, who couldn't come to terms with a decision that this person had made.

"Hamilton, I'm sorry for interrupting, but, you do realize that he's awake," said the woman. It was a soft voice, a sweet voice, and if not for his pounding headache, Collin thought he'd like it.

"Yes, thank you...Collin," said H, "there's a glass of water and a painkiller on the table for you...took quite a knock on the noggin, you're more than likely concussed."

Collin opened his eyes slowly, his stomach turned, he shut them. He took a deep breath, then exhaled while recognizing the scent that hung in the air. He could smell some burning incense, and the aroma of marijuana that still clung to him, but intertwined with them was the musty smell from his ghost story, where someone had watched him shower, then disappeared.

"Collin," said the woman, "I swear, if you shoot or stab me, I'll shove your gun up your ass and your knife up your nose."

"Dee, please...Collin is far too bright to be so foolish. Had he been prepped properly...and I blame myself entirely for all of this. I knew he was loyal to his friends, and I gave him no reason not to accompany them. I should have said something when I cancelled our appointment." explained H.

Collin listened to their words through the pain that each syllable drummed into his head, leaving shards of agony with every beat. He felt like he was going to be sick, and tried to sit up in order to find something to puke in.

He opened his eyes, pain filled the void behind them, Collin's stomach sank, then he tried to say 'help', but nothing came out.

"Here," said Hamilton, taking Collin's hand and placing something small in his palm, "this will fix you right up, try to get it down."

Collin shook his head weakly.

"Let me," said the woman's voice.

Collin felt a hand on his face. A thumb on one cheek, and fingers on the other. They were soft, cold, and were pulling his jaw down. His lips parted, and he felt fingers pushing H's pill into his mouth. Then Collin had a hand on each cheek, and Dee was giving him a kiss. A cold, soft, heart-stopping kiss, that he would have undoubtedly enjoyed, but in his state, Collin was wishing that there was nothing, absolutely nothing that might smell, make noise, or touch him. He just wanted everything to stop and go away. But now there was a hand on the back of his head, and a glass was being held to his lips. Water ran into his mouth until his tongue was submerged.

"Swallow," said Dee, her hand lifted his chin, tilting his head back.

A neck spasm shot bolts of pain into his head as he swallowed, he winced, and tears ran into his ears. Collin took a deep breath, he shuddered, and the air rattled out of his lungs in whimpers.

Deana's icy hand moved to his neck, and she eased him back into the fetal position on the couch. Collin grabbed her wrist when she tried to move her hand, whispering, "feels good..."

He then felt her coolness on his forehead, but it wasn't her other hand, it was her cheek. All that he could smell was her mustiness, but Dee's caress felt so cool and comforting, he didn't mind that she smelled like an old basement.

He felt a warmth spreading through his body, starting in his hands and feet, flowing up his arms and legs. When it reached his chest and head, the pain began to come and go in swells of agony and relief. His migraine then lifted, dissipating through the top of his head like sand through an hourglass. Collin felt his senses returning to him, and he was able to think without it hurting. He didn't feel like he was going to throw up anymore.

The waves of warmth kept pulsating through his system. He felt stronger with each one, until finally, the pain was a distant memory. Collin now felt better that ever, physically and mentally. He was thinking again, and recalling the events that had led to this moment. His distrust and anger now steering his mind.

"What did you give me?" asked Collin.

"Feeling better?" inquired H.

"Uh-huh...so, what did you give me?" repeated Collin.

"Just a little something that we take from time to time to feel a little, invigoration," answered H.

"What's it going to do to me?" asked Collin.

"Oh, nothing permanent, if that's what you're worried about," replied H.

"No? I'm not going to turn into one of those zombies?" asked Collin.

"Oh my no...you're systems have just been recharged...it's a little technical, but rest assured Collin, you'll be fine...better than fine for a while," said H.

"Sure, whatever you say," said Collin.

"I don't think he trusts you Hamilton." said Dee.

"I'm sure you're right, after what the poor man's been through," said H, "although, you certainly held your own, didn't you Collin?"

Collin said nothing, but thought about his knife and gun, and how he could use them now, to find Eric and Mac, and get the hell out of there.

"You didn't kill anyone tonight...only hurt their pride , so don't worry about that," said H.

Collin wasn't worried about it. No, he was only worried that there might not be any way out of his current predicament. He was having difficulties in forming an escape plan. All he knew for sure was that his friends would soon be dead if they weren't already, that there was a new black Camaro somewhere on the farm, that he'd surely die if he tried to save Eric and Mac or get to the car, and that he was still afraid to open his eyes.

"What do I have to do to get me and my friends out of here?"

asked Collin.

"Oh, no...wouldn't you like to stay a while? I was hoping you'd want to pick my brain while we...that's it!" exclaimed H. "We can answer your question with a game of chess, how's that? If you beat me, I'll try to help you get your friends out of here. Fair enough?"

"So they're still alive...what do you want with us?" asked Collin.

"Deana, I'd like to have a word with Collin," hinted H.

"So have them," she replied.

"Please Dee, I'll introduce you properly a little later," insisted H.

"Fine, have your little talk, fill his head with nonsense," huffed Deana as she left the room.

"Thank you Dee...don't mind her Collin, she's a free spirit, and not very interested in the big picture, unlike you and me," said H. "Can you open your eyes?"

"I don't know that I want to," answered Collin through his teeth.

"Now, that is nonsense...I know what you're going through, really, I was in a situation much like yours, once upon a time," said H. "You have a cool head, like myself, and you'll appreciate what I have to say, as I did when I was in your place."

Collin wasn't very concerned with what H had to say, but he was right, he would have to open his eyes, he'd need them to fight, or flee.

He put his open palms up to his face, and slowly opened his eyes behind the safety of his fingers. He was able to open them wide without any sign of a headache, so he opened his fingers, then lowered his hands and took in his surroundings. The lighting was dim, and his eyes adjusted painlessly in an instant.

H was standing, leaning against a huge desk with thick legs that gave it the look of a snooker table. It had a thick smooth flat marble top, which was black as night and streaked with greys and reds.

Behind H were huge glass french doors. Black drapes hung on either side of them, and through them, Collin could see the lake shimmering. He wasn't sure why, but he thought that the water might be his best option for escape.

Above the doors was a pair of swords angled towards each other as though they were about to duel. The ceiling was high, and made up entirely of intricate sculptures, some beautiful, and others grotesque. It was all trimmed with thick white moldings which were also comprised of some madman's artwork. All of the details seemed to have a flow that drew the eyes up to the centre of the ceiling, where, in the midst of piles of bones, skulls and contorted corpses, was a smiling face.

"Ah, yes...that, is Anon. I had this room made to commemorate a great war. It was brief, but it was fierce. Millions lost their lives in the conflict...mostly men...but Anon levelled the playing field and ultimately ended the war, for ever." said H. "Have you ever heard of Anon?"

"Nope, can't say that I have," replied a bitter Collin.

"Anon," said H, "is a God, if ever there was one. He didn't create the universe, not intentionally anyways, but it was born because of him...I've met him you know."

So, he's a name dropper, Collin thought to himself. "A God. really," he said without much interest. He'd left Hamilton's last night thinking about alien's, and tonight it would be gods. What about werewolves and zombie vampires? He wouldn't mind hearing an explanation for those.

"Yes, a God, absolutely," confirmed H proudly, "and it would seem that he's leaving. He's grown tired of this batch of humanity. You see, he's very fond of man, but he's tired of being disappointed. He's tried to impart wisdom and help in more ways and times than you can imagine. But, it only takes one to ruin the lot, or so he says. The pathology of some men make them conquerors of other men and all that they have. I believe that Anon's vision of a utopia is lost on humans. They are a fad of ignorance and selfishness that could never even hope to suppress their...I'm sorry Collin...I've been known to rant. Tell me Collin, would you like to live forever?"

Collin couldn't believe that Hamilton was trying to have a conversation, like nothing had happened, and all was right as rain. "Forever eh, doubtful," he said.

"Really, why not?" inquired H.

"Well, if you mean forever, as in, till the end of time, then, that's never, right? Would I want to live to see the end of everything, the death of the universe, and keep on keeping on?

No thanks," said Collin.

"I see your point," said H, "and that is exactly what Anon has to wrestle with."

"So, where is this God going to go if he's so fond of humans?" asked Collin, slightly intrigued, but also trying to buy some time so that he could think of a way to get the best of Hamilton.

"Ah, yes. Well, I'm told that he plans to start over, somewhere else, with some of his favourites," said H.

"Start over?" asked Collin.

"Absolutely. I think it would mean that he plans to populate another planet, and give humanity another go," said H, through a laugh, because the idea amused him.

"What? Another planet? And, uh, how would he get his, uh, favourites to this new planet?" asked Collin, slightly amused himself.

"Anon would simply make it so Collin. He is not a man, though he enjoys pretending to be one. He is a most powerful being, capable of manipulating all of existence," said H.

"Ok. Is he planning on taking you with him?" inquired Collin.

"Alas, no...heck no," said H, then chuckled as though it was a funny concept, but Collin thought that he saw a sadness in H, in his brow, and in his eyes.

"I don't get it. You know a God, he knows you...how many people know this guy?" asked Collin. "Why wouldn't he take you?"

Hamilton flinched ever so slightly, then said, "As I was saying, mankind is his hobby."

"You're not a man...so H, what are you?" asked Collin, now sensing that Hamilton, who was still leaning against the desk, with his hands gripping it's edges, might have a vulnerability.

"No," said H with a smile, "not anymore. I was a man, millenniums ago. It isn't uncommon for Anon to settle a new colony, he's done it before. "

"Right...so, you're from another planet..." said Collin with a smirk.

"Right,"said H, "technically, so are you. Almost two hundred thousand years ago, people carrying your genetics travelled here with Anon. Our ancestors were from another world. Anyhow, I was a man, the descendant of generations of great men who lived light-years away, then here on earth." said H, still smiling.

"But, this Anon guy changed you?" asked Collin.

"Oh, no...no no. Anon had nothing to do with that. I was infected by a woman. I believe that she was infected by her husband, who had stumbled upon a fallen meteorite, or was bitten himself. I believe this because Anon has suggested that 'vampirism' is caused by a parasite that survives for only a brief moment, unless it finds a host of course. It's like a virus. He has seen it elsewhere, on other planets, and he's witnessed it among all animals, not only man." explained Hamilton. "In the right body, these organisms can sustain life for thousands of years.

But in most, it takes over, and the inhabited become hollow feeders, living only a few days, to kill and drink...they're animals, beasts." said H.

"Speaking of living to drink, I still don't know where the boys are," said Collin. He'd forgotten about them for a moment while Hamilton told his tale.

"Mmmm. Max and Eric are here for...training, let's say." said H, his smile disappearing. "How long would you like to live Collin, if it were up to you?"

"Obsess much?" replied Collin.

"Excuse me!" hissed Hamilton, not expecting the tone that had just been used against him. But he then realized that it could be a good thing. Collin was displaying a strong character, he would face what he had to without complaint, and on his own terms.

"Immortality," said Collin, "you seem to be trying to snag a hook in my brain with it. I don't know what to tell you. It's all relevant, right...if I was always going to be this age, in good shape and all, I'm sure I'd appreciate a few hundred years. But, if I was a curse, or just some form of eternal energy...I don't know, what would be the point of living forever if you're not really living?"

"Only a few hundred? Do you think that you'd tire of this world?" asked H.

"When can I see Eric and Mac?" asked Collin.

"Obsess much?" smiled H. "I really don't think that's a good idea. No, not at all."

"Why's that?" asked Collin.

"They're being...interviewed. I am sorry Collin, really. You weren't supposed to know anything about this." answered H.

"Yeah, well, I do know about it." said Collin.

"Fine. I'll take you to see them, in a while. But, the deal's been done, I have no say over what happens to them now." said H.

"But, you just wanted to bet me for them. Chess, remember?" said Collin.

"Yes. You're right. I shouldn't have done that. If you'd have won, I could not have held up my end of the bargain." said H.

"H. You seem to want me to trust you. Am I right? Try telling me some truths. Am I going to see the boys again, alive?" pleaded Collin.

"You're loyalty is more than admirable Collin. And I mean that. You're being more honourable than you should be. Without you, those two would have been imprisoned or killed long ago. From a business stand-point, we had to get them off the streets. In fact, the only thing that's kept them working for the past year was your friend's insistence that you could keep them in line," said Hamilton, leaving his desk and slowly walking from window to window. "Personally, I didn't think that it was very fair to you, but if viewed as a test of character, you've more than proven yourself...more..."

"Why do you want them gone so bad?" asked Collin.

"Are you fuckin' serious? Collin, from day one they've been untrustworthy, unpredictable and accident prone, oh, and I shouldn't forget to mention, dumb and dangerous." said Hamilton, running a finger down a statue that stood between two windows. It looked like it had a Samurai's armour, with curved blades hooking out of it's plating. This statue, unlike all the others, didn't have a weapon as far as Collin could see.

"And, you couldn't have just let them go, fired them, so to speak...cut them off?", asked Collin.

"No. Think about it. Best case scenario, they go out in a blaze of glory robbing a liquor store or in a stand-off with the police. Worst case scenario, they spill their guts for a little leniency. You'd be the first to go down with them Collin. And that's where it would end. Matthew would survive it, so would I, but you'd take the heat for everything they've done," said H sternly. "Have I skipped a scenario? Am I missing a piece of the puzzle? Would they have straightened themselves out, become bank managers, or school teachers?"

"Guess I didn't realize how far up the chain they'd pissed," said Collin, "seriously, what's going to happen to them?"

"Ok. Collin, we operate a hobby farm here. And like any ecosystem we have a food chain. The workers tend to the plants, we bring in pickers once a year, and when they're done with the harvest, they feed the workers. The workers, if you're wondering, are the 'zombies' that you referred to. They'll live a year without much food, and are fantastic servants. They do, mind you, tend to get a little feral after seven or eight years, so, we have to put them down, and replace them of course. If your friends survive the night, they will likely find themselves tending the fields for Stephan." explained Hamilton.

"If they survive the night..." repeated Collin.

"Stephan is not to be crossed. If one of your friends fails to recognize this and disrespects him beyond his tolerances, he will put them down without a second thought." said H.

"And you have no control over Stephan, is that it?" asked Collin.

"No, not really. If I ask him nicely, sometimes he goes out of his way for me, but for the most part, he tells me to fuck off," H laughed and shrugged, "his role is to protect the farm and it's inhabitants, including myself, and he does it exceptionally well. Stephan would put his life on the line to save mine, it's in his nature...but favours are not. If I were to ask him to go back on our deal, he'd tear out their throats just so he could laugh about it. Hopefully, your friends learn quickly...and don't make any derogatory comments about Frenchmen."

"So there's nothing I can say or do to get to Eric and Mac? And you won't intervene?" invited Collin.

"There is a history between my people and the wolves. We are bound to each-other and the rules that govern us. Stephan is an odd one. His predecessor was a very pleasant and agreeable man, but Stephan is a wild-card. He doesn't want anything. It makes it impossible to sway him on anything... he's very stubborn, and he takes pleasure in frustrating others. None of his underlings would dare oppose me, but he has no fear, and when it comes to his pack, he is alpha absolute."

"So, I should just forget about them, take a tour of your

mansion...pick out a room." mused Collin.

"Collin," said Hamilton glancing at an old clock, "in a couple of hours the wolves will have segregated the future workers from the fodder. They make a game of it. It takes a few hours, and ends at midnight with the death of the runts, so to speak. They will open the doors at the killing hour, for our viewing pleasure. Until then there is nothing that I can do, so please, Collin, I beseech you, enough is enough, I don't want to hear about them anymore. I don't know how else to say it. I will not interfere with Stephan's affairs, I'm sorry that it's come to this, but you're going to have to rise to the occasion."

Collin thought about rising alright. Rising and lunging, blade in hand, swiping once, upwards, across Hamilton's throat, then back down into his temple. From there he could cut off his head or gouge out his heart, then take a shit on H's desk, right in the middle of it, centrepieces are always a nice touch.

"Well," said Hamilton, "how's about that tour?"

Collin let his gaze meet Hamilton's for the first time in a while. He was somewhat at odds with himself, since he liked H's company, for the most part, but he so wanted to slit his throat and cut out his tongue.

"This, as you know, is the war room. I meant to have it filled with remnants from the battle I spoke of earlier, the battle of Tess, or, Tesan Uvol. This," said H as he walked to the statue that lacked a weapon, "is Tess. He was my master. He was going to kill me, because he hadn't turned me...we met when I was feeding in what he felt was his territory. He was the one who put me through my trials. He was the one who made me prove myself worthy. I don't know that we were ever very close, but I was grateful to him for showing me how to survive...I didn't know that I was a vampire, I thought that I was mad, that I'd gone insane...imagine, all the allergies, and the thirst, but not knowing why, and trying to maintain a social life...I was a raving lunatic. Yessir, and Tess took me in..." H trailed off.

"He was a warrior?" inquired Collin, wanting to keep Hamilton on a roll.

"A warrior, yes. He led us against the army of men who meant to exterminate us. Millions against a few thousand of us. Tesan fought like a devil, slicing twenty men in half with one flick of his wrist." Hamilton nodded towards the long thin sword that hung on the back wall. Eight feet long, at least, with a slight curve in it from the hilt to the tip. "That was his weapon of choice. Made of what we called 'Sessa', it would translate roughly to 'master of all'. I call it diamond-glass. It'll cut through anything, with the right person wielding it."

"Is that what he looked like, or is that a mask?" asked Collin, noticing the big eyes and snarled lips revealing fangs.

"It's meant to be a likeness of him," said H.

"He died in this battle?" probed Collin.

"He did. One minute he was gliding through an endless sea of men, cutting them down like flowers...then he was a cloud of red...dust...he was gone, just like that." said H.

"I don't get it," urged Collin.

"Anon. He was watching the battlefield. I don't know why he

let it go on as long as it did, or why he let it happen at all...but at some point, he ended it by killing most of my comrades. He did it with a thought, nothing more. It was awesome." said Hamilton.

"Why didn't he kill you?" asked Collin.

"He knew my grandfather, and met me as a child. He recognized me, same goes for the other survivors. He's very sentimental when it comes to man." offered H.

"He ended the battle without a clear victor? Why didn't he wipe you out? It doesn't make sense," said Collin.

"Oh, the victory would have been ours had Anon not meddled, of that I have no doubt. He meant to wipe us out, but I think he decided that it wouldn't be fair. What he said was that fighting nature should be the measure of hopelessness. He is fond of man, and helps him at the risk of upsetting the natural order of things, and it weighs on him. It was suggested that we are a natural progression of man, and he could not argue it, but it bothered him nonetheless. Anon taught me to...keep a low profile. Well, I am certain that his bright plan for my survival is also beneficial to man, wouldn't you agree? I believe that it was a suggestion on his part, and a threat as well. He was indicating that he would tolerate us within certain boundaries. We could share the planet, or be cleansed from it," said H. "I think that he's content with how we manage ourselves."

"Yay for me," said Collin.

"You will thank me one day, mark my words Collin," said H, "now, the battle of Tess was fought a hundred and twenty thousand years ago. It was a miracle that even the few objects I have survived and were reclaimed. Many of the other artifacts are from more recent civilizations. As much as I wanted to dedicate this room to the war and to Anon, I simply did not have enough treasures from that era to properly decorate it. What is even sadder is that the technologies that were lost have yet to be rediscovered."

"Right. And, uh, why wouldn't you have helped to 'rediscover' them?" asked Collin, "I mean, if you have lost technologies squirrelled away in your brain, why wouldn't you? You'd rule the world for Christ's sake."

"Collin, who said that we don't rule the world? Besides, would you empower your enemy? Consider this. When I lived as a man, it was among a people that was united on a journey to enlightenment. It was a world of cooperation and daily achievement. I have yet to read a book or watch a movie that portrays a futuristic civilization that comes close to capturing how I once lived." said H.

"Maybe you should move to Hollywood, become a director, make your movie," said a slightly sarcastic Collin.

"Uh-huh...maybe I should. In any case, we didn't war with each-other...and I'm not pulling your leg. We had no reason for warriors, much less armies. I can go into it more later, but my point was, the world is simply not ready for the responsibility that would come with being able to harness the kind of power we're talking about here." stated Hamilton.

"Last night, you said that there was no hope for man. But now, you're saying man was nothing but hope...a hundred and twenty thousand years ago," pointed out Collin.

"Man is not the animal it once was. It will never be ruled the way it was then. Life was a duty back then...and not to oneself Collin. The last thing one considered was themselves. However, by today's standards, it was a highly brainwashed society I suppose. Very...totalitarian." said H.

"Ok. So, what happened to your great civilization?" asked Collin.

"Ice happened Collin. A few generations after the war, the climate started to change. They had forecasts and models of future conditions globally, and so, people congregated to the areas that were believed to be safe-havens. The models were mostly accurate. A few billion survived for a while, before resources became scarce. It wasn't difficult for areas that didn't freeze and already had some sort of infrastructure. But, many areas were arid to start with, and the refugees died out quickly. I thought I was going to be safe. There was a city, just there," H pointed out the window at the Great Lake. "Ice just scraped it off the face of the planet. Anyways, in the devastation was born a new people. The ones who had lost their infrastructures, and had to scavenge and kill to survive...they changed all the rules. Living then was a helluva thing, and many people lost their minds, killed themselves, and worse. I was used to feeding...but when I saw cannibalism for the first time, it changed something in me." said H, walking slowly to the door, "and it changed something in men. Centuries of scarcity twisted generations of wandering, warring pockets of survivors into the descendents that you see now. Everyone is born with a memory Collin. The blueprint of an ancestral knowledge is embedded in each mind...am I boring you?"

"No, no, not at all...we going somewhere?" inquired Collin.

"I thought I could show you around, we still have some time to kill," said Hamilton.

Collin finished off the glass of water then made his way around the room to look at some of the artifacts that had caught his eye. A double ended blade that was in the same style as the long sword that Tess had wielded. An eight inch double edge at each end. There was another piece that had attracted him as well. A long jacket that hung on the same wall as the door. It was framed, like a jersey or butterfly collection. It was the same colour as the knife and sword. A strange black that had a sheen like glass. Collin had seen a geological display once, and it reminded him of one of the rocks that was in it. He couldn't remember what it was called, but it looked like black ice.

"That was Tess' overcoat," said H, "it's made of diamond-glass as well, woven, just like any textile. Tesan was rarely without it...the sword and dagger sheaths are built into it...beautiful, isn't it?"

"Yes, yes it is," replied Collin, who was picturing himself in it, and liking what he saw. "Do you ever wear it?"

Hamilton looked at the hanging coat and said, "absolutely not. Tesan died wearing it, and brandishing it's weapons. We found a few other piles of armour and clothing, but Anon destroyed all traces of the majority of my brethren. Why he left a few, including this one intact, I can't say, I've asked him many questions, but his answers are often questions in themselves.

I've often wondered if it was the diamond-glass. Perhaps it inhibits him somehow."

"Maybe, not enough to save the guy wearing it though," said Collin, still admiring the intricately stitched jacket. It looked like it had never been worn, but he suspected that the garment saw it's fair share of action.

"Right. To fully answer your question, no, I believe it to be haunted Collin. I donned it once, and never will again. And, I'm not the only one who has felt and feared it's dark embrace," said H, "now, how about a tour that puts all the museums to shame, come...can I get you something to drink?"

"No, thanks," said Collin, wanting both hands to be free. He followed Hamilton out of the war room, through it's arched doorway, into a hallway that stretched a hundred feet in either direction. It too was lined with statues of warriors and demon-like characters. The floor and walls were a white marble, contrasted by the same dark marble as Hamilton's desk, and more artwork was chiseled into it everywhere that he looked. Each had a story to tell, he was sure, and wondered how long this tour was going to take, and how many others were wandering around the mansion. "Hey, I keep seeing that symbol everywhere...on armour and weapons, on your walls, the ceilings, floors," said Collin, pointing at a swirl on one of the armour's shoulders, then at a few more in the artwork, "it reminds me of fiddle-heads, you know, the plant that some people eat...or one of those big lollipops."

"Mmmm, the spiral. It's funny Collin, how I just take some things for granted. That, my friend, is the circle of life. Ends do not meet on life's journeys. Everything spirals, into or out of control, into beginning or end...mmmm...I apologize, the symbol has many meanings, as most do." said H.

"Alright, well, what's it mean to you?" inquired Collin.

"Everything ends," said H.

"Everything ends," repeated Collin.

"I like your fiddle-head analogy," said Hamilton, stepping towards the wall, touching a sculpted spiral at it's base. "Is this the beginning, or the end? Does it matter? It's just a coiled line...all lines have ends," he said, tracing his finger along the spiral's groove.

"Uh, little demoralizing, no," said Collin.

"Well, it depends on who you ask. If you want a fancier version, talk to Deana, symbols are near and dear to her," offered H. "Stephan says it's all 'stupide'. That, if it's meant to represent the lives of men, then man traps himself, corners himself into retracing his steps till he dies. It can mean anything Collin, the thing to take away from it is, you must take advantage of the life you have, now, before the spiral ends."

"Of course...or...your ancestors just really liked fiddle-heads," said Collin.

Hamilton chuckled, "absolutely," he said. "This is going to be a fun tour. You ready? Let us begin."

∞

10

Friday night, sitting in a fine chair on a patio overlooking the waters of Lake Huron. It was calm, peaceful even, with eight or nine other people taking advantage of the weather and locale. Collin counted them now, five men and four women, drinking from their small white bottles, sitting, like him, in comfy wicker chairs, sharing stories, reminiscing and laughing like they were at a small sidewalk cafe.

Hamilton's words still echoed in Collin's mind, and were being processed by it as well as they could. The tour he'd just taken didn't include anything that he'd always considered to be history. Like a fish out of water, nothing felt right anymore. He couldn't be certain of anything at all. Hamilton had shown him proof of every type of monster and fairy tale creature he'd ever heard of, which only made up a quarter of the ones H had spoken of. Man's history, according to H, spanned hundreds of thousands of years, and multiple planets. Whatever it was that H was up to, Collin was now fully aware that he knew less than nothing, and it was so unsettling that he thought he felt that damned migraine making a comeback. The earthy must that filled his sinuses wasn't helping his nausea either, it was sickening.

He realized that there was one thing that mattered here tonight, no matter what Hamilton's story. Whatever the realities that were going to be exposed to him, no matter how stupid and uncomfortable things got here, Collin would maintain an air of calm and show his host nothing but respect. Being polite will get you a long way, even with the strangest of characters.

"Can I ask you something?" inquired Collin.

"Anything, please," said H.

"Was it you, or someone else, one of your friends here who watched me while I showered?" Collin asked, realizing that he'd just told himself to be polite.

"Ah, yes...it's the odor, isn't it? Dead giveaway I'm told. I wonder, does anyone pick up on their own smell? Doubtful I suppose. In any case, no Collin, it wasn't me, and I can't tell you if it was someone that I know. I can't tell you something that I do not know." replied H.

Collin nodded, he believed Hamilton, and was about to tell him so, when he heard the sweetest voice there was.

"It was me," said Deana from behind him.

Collin recognized her voice, and stood to get a better look at her. She was sitting with another woman and a man. She stood, then walked towards Collin, passed him, and stood beside Hamilton who was still sitting, smiling, with curiosity on his brow. Deana crossed her arms and took in Collin from head to toe.

"I must say, you aren't nearly as sickly as I remember you. It's nice to see you again," said the most stunningly beautiful woman that had ever spoken to Collin. She was of average height, and had light brown hair. Her bangs were cut straight across and hid most of her eyebrows. The sides hung to her jaw, then tapered down to the base of her neck. Collin now took her in, from head to toe. She was amazing. Deana was thin with boyish hips, but with a bust that set her apart from any boy. Dressed in a yellow sundress, her long, toned and shapely legs were incredible too, but, it was her lips and eyes that he fell a little bit in love with in that moment. Full, pouting lips that he knew to be soft. Eyes that sparkled. They looked dark, but light danced in them like it was alive, and Collin caught himself re-organizing the night's priorities while gazing into them.

"Collin," said H, "let me introduce you to Deana...she's lovely, isn't she?"

Collin nodded in agreement, lost for words.

Hamilton stood from his seat, and stepped to Collin's side. He raised his left hand to Collin's chin and gently pushed Collin's jaw up. "There," said H through a chuckle, "let me get that for you."

"Dee, sweetie, you know my young friend, do you?" asked H.

"No. He caught my eye not too long ago. I thought he was handsome. I followed him home," said Deana, holding Collin's gaze with her own.

"You watched me shower...disappeared," mumbled Collin.

Deana shifted her stance from one foot to the other. She

straightened her back and shoulders. "I was going to feed on him," she admitted to Hamilton, "but he was toxic, with medications I think. I wanted him...but his blood was tainted...his organs were shutting down. I'm delighted to see you again Collin, and with such a glow...how long ago was it, the night that I watched you shower?"

"Uh, not sure...two and a half, maybe three years ago," replied a very self-conscious Collin.

"Collin here," explained H, "has Alopecia, which is why he is so beautifully bald. You are correct my dear, he was on many prescriptions, for as many symptomatic issues. But it was Collin himself, who, using his keen logic and rationale, came to understand that only he and his will could remedy his toxic situation. Isn't that right Collin?" smiled H.

"Uhm, good food...nutrients, juicing...lifestyle change...I feel good," stammered Collin, blushing. He wasn't used to this kind of attention, especially from a beautiful woman. Deana was enchanting him right down to the marrow. He couldn't stop staring into her big eyes. He tried to break away every once in a while, to look at nothing in particular, but would return to them within seconds, to fixate on them, and lose himself in them.

"Isn't this interesting," said H, "I know exactly what incident it is you're talking about. Dee, Collin told me about it just last night while playing chess. Incredible, isn't it? Dee was going to kill you Collin, how about that? And, it turns out, you're only alive today because you were sick then...amazing. And here you stand today. Good enough to eat, and if I have my say, good enough to be one of us."

Hamilton put his hand on Collin's shoulder and smiled at him, then he looked at Deana. "I'm not surprised that you followed him that night. I wish that you were meeting under better circumstances. I'm pretty sure that Collin has been thinking about misbehaving. He'd still like to use his knife on us all."

"That would be a pity. I can still taste his lips," said Deana, "can you still taste mine? You don't want your death to be a feeding, do you?" She exaggerated her pout. "Wouldn't you like to get to know me? You're not really going to hurt me, are you?"

Collin didn't know what to say. He hadn't once thought about hurting Deana. How could he? She was magnificent, and she was showing interest in him. He'd been waiting for a moment, an opening to spring into action, but the more he heard and saw, the less opportune the moments seemed to get. In fact, for the last few, Collin had been daydreaming about the lovely creature that was standing a few feet from him.

"I must apologize to you as well my dear," said H to Deana, "if not for my lapse in foresight, you might have Collin's undivided attention. But, I fear that his friends, Eric and Max, who delivered the new Camaro, are distracting him from the moment."

"Ooou...the new Camaro," cooed Deana, still staring deeply into Collin's eyes. "Is it black, like I requested?" she asked.

"Absolutely," replied Hamilton.

"Mmmm...how amazing would you look driving a car like that?" said Deana to Collin, raising one eyebrow and smiling seductively. "Or, driving me in a car like that?"

Collin felt himself blushing again. His heart skipped then took on a new, quicker rhythm. His legs felt numb, and his left knee was shaking, trembling. He put his hands on his hips and took a deep breath, puffing his chest out and pushing his shoulders back, hoping to distract from the two-step that he was doing because of his weak knees. He made a few odd, even funny faces while trying to say something. He opened his mouth, but couldn't think of anything but Deana, her sundress, and what was hidden underneath it. He clasped his hands together and said, "Ah," then grimaced again, and nodded profusely in agreement with himself. He opened his hands, held them out palms up, and shrugged, saying, "Yep...yeah, but no..." then he thought of something. "They...Eric and MaC...not Max," he said, emphasizing his friends name, "they delivered the Camaro. It was a twofer, they deliver the car, and you have your way with them."

"Well, ya," said H.

Collin shook his head in frustration, "they looked so damned happy driving out here...poor bastards."

"Collin, seriously, can you please explain to me what it is that compels you to care about those two, I'm at a loss." said H.

Collin opened his mouth to answer, but nothing was said. It wasn't coming to him as quickly as he'd hoped. In his retrospection, he wondered if it was less about Eric and Mac, and more about himself, and how he'd been duped. He was the leader of the misfit trio, and he'd been intentionally snookered, he couldn't help them...he was having difficulties in reasoning why he felt obligated to them, other than, he knew them, and babysat them for a few years.

"It's because they're yours," said Deana. "We all want to protect our own."

"Yeah, that's partly it. I did have some good times with them you know." said Collin.

"Name one," challenged Hamilton.

Once again Collin was at a loss. He wracked his mind for a memory of them all having a good time together. Most of what he recalled was work related, and the rest involved them being high, getting into trouble, and Collin having to make things right.

"I don't know," said Collin, "I've had some good laughs with them...or, at their expense maybe."

"Care to share a story or two?" asked Deana.

"Oh, I can't think of anything that would be...suitable," replied Collin.

"Suitable?" asked Hamilton.

"Well, there's one story that stands out. It's always good for a laugh...but, there's a lady present, and it's a story for boys, ya know, a poop story," said Collin.

"Collin, I'm a big girl, I can handle more than you can imagine," said Deana.

Collin looked at Deana, then at Hamilton, then decided that

maybe he could help them see that Eric and Mac were just big kids, and that there might be a better way to deal with them. He realized though that the story that he was about to tell might only solidify the idea that they are useless.

"Ok, but I'm warning you, it's not pretty," said Collin.

"Give us all you got kiddo," said H.

"Fine. Well, it was about two years ago. We'd had a few decent paying jobs and some downtime on our hands. I was doing my thing, and they were doing theirs, getting high at Madame Kitty's, or on a rooftop, or in an alley somewhere. Well, one day, they stop by my place and they want to use the car. Hooch got us a little Hyundai, it's a part of a fleet, anyways, I usually have the keys, and they wanted to borrow them."

Collin took a sip from the glass of water that sat on the patio table then continued, "Turns out, the place where they've been hanging out, Kitty's, had some dog handling marathon on t.v., and all the junkies and hoes there went dog crazy. Their interests change every week. Anyhoo, Mac had spoken with some guy that had a dog he was trying to get rid of, I can't remember the reason, but, they all thought it would be sweet to give this dog a new home."

"I met the dog a few times before they got rid of it. It's name was Eddie. It was a mutt, husky and shepherd I think, but it was a brindle colour, very nice, great temperament, but real dumb, you know. But uh, yeah, at the time, I really didn't think that it was a good idea. As I'm sure you know, they aren't exactly responsible. But, uh, they weren't going to take no for an answer, and, not really wanting to deal with them, I handed the keys over. Good thing I did too, cause it's about to get funny."

"They take the car out of the city through some familiar areas on their way to meet this guy with the dog. Well, they decide to stop in and see an old friend who just happens to sell dope. They both love heroin, coke, weed, whatever...there's an occasion for everything, right. The guy is dry, he's got nothing for them, except some peyote. Yeah. It's all he's got, and he warns them...they better be parked for a day if they're going to eat any."

"That just sounds fantastic to the boys, and being true to themselves, they chewed some down on the way to pick up the dog. I guess they figured that they'd be back by the time it kicked in, or that they could handle it. They make it there, they meet the guy, they like the dog, dude gave them all the dog's food and toys, then they pack it up and head back with their new dopey pet."

"They're about five minutes from where they picked it up, which is the middle of nowhere, right. Well, the peyote kicks in, and the boys are fucked...higher than kites, and their bodies, their organs go haywire on them. Eric pulls the car over on the side of the highway, jumps out, runs to the passenger's side, yanks down his pants and, uh, poops on the road."

"You can say shit Collin...or fuck, I'm not a princess," said Deana.

"Ok," continued Collin, " Well, Eric is having the, uh, shit of his life, while Mac on the other hand, is leaning out of the car, right beside Eric, and he's puking his brains out. From what I heard, it sounded like it went on for a while. Shittin' and pukin' in broad daylight while cars are passing by."

" Sooo, they start feeling a little better, and Eric says that he needs something to wipe his ass with, right. He asks Mac for his shirt, he says no. Socks? Nope. Pant-leg, anything? Use your own fuckin' shirt, right?"

"Well, that was enough to get the brawl started. Side of the road, one's covered in puke, the other still has his pants down, they're both out of their minds, hallucinating I'd imagine, and rolling around, scrapping because, well, because they're idiots."

"This goes on for who knows how long. I've seen them torment and piss each-other off, and fight it out for hours at a time. Anyways, they tire themselves out, or come down some, and they patch things up, laugh about it and how fucked up they are. They head back to the car, and there it is...there's Eddie, laying in what was a big puddle of puke, and it's eating Eric's shit!"

Deana's jaw dropped and Hamilton cringed.

"Yeah," went on Collin, "no joke. The dog ate up all the puke, then laid down in it's puddle and ate the poop," he said while struggling not to laugh.

"They drive back a good hour, with this massive dog covered in barf and breathing, no, no...panting it's shit-breath all over them. Oh man, they both got sick in the car, all over themselves, and the car. They stopped a few times to try and get it out of their systems, but as soon as they got back in the car, they'd start dry-heaving again...the whole way back," laughed Collin, "got more stories like that about them than you can imagine."

"So, they amuse you," said H, chuckling.

"Oh yeah," said Collin.

"That was a very funny story, don't you think Dee?" smiled H.

"Disgusting," she said, both hands covering her mouth.

"I warned you," said Collin, "and, we won't get anymore stories like that if you let them both die tonight, eh?"

"Speaking of which, I believe it's almost that time. Shall we?" said H.

"Shall we what?" asked Collin.

Hamilton, who was still standing beside a frowning Collin, looked across the way, to Collin's left, and nodded. "Everyone has left. I don't think that you should bare witness, but if you must, the kennels are that way. That's where everyone has gone. The fate of your friends will have been decided by now, and if one, or both of them are to die, it will be now."

"What? The kennels?" demanded Collin.

"I'll take you," said Deana, who now looked at Collin tenderly, sadly.

"I think I should be with you, if you decide to go," said H.

"What are we waiting for?" blurted Collin before heading off in the direction that H had pointed out.

Collin thought about Deana while he walked hurriedly down

a stone footpath. He also thought about how Hamilton had been toying with him all this time. Deana kept his pace, and stayed by his side while H took up the rear. He was being led away from the mansion, south, along the lake-shore where there wasn't any lighting. When the path merged with bush, and both sides of the path were lined with trees, Collin couldn't see a thing. Walking with his hands outstretched, feeling for trees, he couldn't even see them out in front of his face, but he kept walking.

He heard a muffled cry coming from somewhere up ahead, then cheering. He stepped faster, harder, wondering what it was that he was about to behold. He didn't have a good feeling about it, and his stomach was tightening. He was upset, angry, spooked, mystified and scared, but he was still calm. He wondered if he was still on autopilot. That's how he'd felt for the past couple of hours, like his mind and body were in neutral, because he was in disbelief or shock.

The fact that he had the wits to question his state of mind reassured him that he had some control at least. He thought that he was starting to feel himself again, and that he could raise hell with confidence if need be. Once the boys saw him, they'd have some fight in them too.

Collin heard another cry coming from up the path. It sounded like someone was pleading and screaming for mercy, and it was met with laughter and applause. Another scream rang out, and Collin made out, "please Stop!", in amongst some wordless cries. A chill ran up his spine and goosebumps broke out on his arms. It was a familiar voice that was in distress, that, or his mind was playing tricks on him.

"Collin, keep in mind that you have no control over what happens in here. You'll have a choice to make later, but for now, Stephan is in charge," said H.

There was a light shining through the trees further up the path. As he got closer, Collin could see that the light was sitting above the doors of a barn like structure. He was being led to a big white barn. They called it the kennels. In it someone screamed again, and the crowd cheered.

"Try to minimize any quick movements while we're in the kennels. As a matter of fact, try not to draw any attention to yourself," cautioned Hamilton.

"Aren't you the boss around here?" asked Collin.

"I suppose you could say that. But Stephan and his horde are not to be trifled with. Don't disrespect him in front of his followers...he can be a real asshole. And Collin, please, don't arm yourself. This is unprecedented...I can't be certain how they'll react to you...although Stephan does know about you." said H.

They soon reached the barn, and Deana pushed open one of the two big doors. It was closed behind them by a scrawny, sickly woman. She bowed her head, "Masters" she said, and waved them in. Collin saw her sniffing at the air, and noticed her eyeing his neck. With drool glistening down her chin, she said, "Masters...enjoy."

"AHHH...PLEASE, NO...oh, fuck me...NO, NO NO!!" screamed a voice from within the barn. It's echo was soon followed by a thunderous cheer and stomping, which reverberated through the walls and floor. It was Eric's voice, Collin was sure of it.

"Sounds like we're just in time," said H.

"Collin," said Deana sweetly, "maybe we should head back to the house. Everything that happens can be retold. There is no need for you to see your friends in pain...believe me, it's the kind of thing that stays with you for a long time."

He knew that she was probably right. But he couldn't stop moving forward. He didn't want to see what was happening to his friend, but he wouldn't stop trying to be there for him. It was his fault that tonight had happened. He'd let it all unfold knowing that something was off. He should have put and end to it in Hooch's office when he had the chance. He should have gotten in the car with them. He should have slit Hamilton's neck hours ago and busted the boys out...he should of kept going down the highway with his trailer in tow, and not looked back.

They were walking down a corridor, and Deana had taken the lead. They passed an office on their left, and a locker room on their right, then Deana turned to her left through a doorway that led to a stairwell. Collin and H followed her up to the barn's next level, where it opened up to a seating gallery where a dozen well-dressed men and women were watching the show, and a few others were having conversations like they were sitting through the coming attractions.

As they descended the steps to the front of the observation deck, growls and snapping sounds, accompanied by wet slapping turned Collin's stomach a little more. He felt light headed when he saw the white walls below him, spattered and streaked with blood. And as he took his final steps down to the railing, he got a full view of the walls, which were so stained by so much blood, they were nearly black in some spots.

He was overlooking a scene that made him want to wretch. Blood was everywhere, it was so thick in the air that he could taste it. It was so surreal that he felt distant from it while trying to process it. What he was taking in felt like it had already happened, like he was watching a movie. A horror movie, and the crew had gone all out on this one. Maximum gore and special effects, good ones too, the best that Collin had ever seen.

He stood at the edge of the killing floor, watching groups of walking corpses lining the room's walls, huddled along three of them, five, six deep in places. The other wall had a grand circular window, and below it, a big wooden throne, and sitting in it was a werewolf. It was as black as tar, except for silver streaks in it's beard and around it's ears. It looked bored, one leg slung over an armrest, picking at it's teeth with a long claw.

In the middle of the room was the thing that was occupying everyone's attention. It was a legless man trying to ward off what looked like werewolf pups. Three nasty little fur-balls were lunging at him, jaws gnashing, fangs sinking deep into his flesh. The man howled in pain while trying to inflict as much damage to his attackers as he could, and hold his guts in place, which were trying to spill out.

It still didn't feel real, and Collin blankly scanned the room for something that made sense, something that he could relate to and ground him somehow. The fog only lifted from his mind for a moment, when reality searched him out. "COLLIN!"

shrieked the shredded man writhing around on the floor staring wide-eyed up at him.

And with a familiar 'click' in the back of his mind, it all registered. "Eric," muttered Collin, in time to see a pup tare out his throat and gobble it down like it was a bacon treat.

The pups kept feeding as the screaming stopped. Their meal was still thrashing around, pointlessly trying to defend itself and stop the blood from squirting out of it's neck simultaneously. It's eyes though, did not leave Collin's. And when they grew dim, when the life left Eric's eyes, Collin realized that every other set in the room were on him too.

He looked into the faces of werewolves, their cubs, and ghoulish looking things that could have been vampires, but looked more like zombies. Behind him were other pretty ones, like Hamilton and Deana, and he knew that they were watching him as well. There must have been eighty of them in all. Collin couldn't remember how many Hamilton said lived on the farm, if he did, but it looked like many of them were attending his friend's mutilation.

All eyes were on him, and it was so quiet that he could hear his heart beating. The room spun and his vision blurred for an uncomfortable second or two. He now felt like he was watching himself while he gestured to the crowd with a small wave and said, "nice night for a party."

After another uncomfortable silence, laughter arose from the kennels' killing room floor. A cacophony of maniacal laughs and howls and of stomping feet was the soundtrack that Collin would remember when recalling one of the cubs choking up some of Eric as it laughed.

He thought that he was going to throw up, maybe even defecate. He was pulling a whitey and he was completely sober. 'First time for everything,' he thought as the room tilted again. Collin felt like he might faint, and he did eventually, right after he noticed someone in the mob, someone who was not laughing. He was staring at the mess on the ground. It was Mac, he was still alive, he was crying, and he looked like hell. He peered up at Collin and sobbed, then Collin folded in half and fell into a shock induced sleep, and Deana's waiting arms.

∞

11

Collin's mind swam through one disturbing dream after another. Dark, creepy crawly nightmares that oozed with a black slickness. Animal eyes, fur, fangs and drool watched him as he stood over a heap of dismembered corpses, and all the parts were moving. Like waves rolling into each other, the pile of bodies churned and roiled in a hypnotic death-roll. He saw everyone he'd ever known in that pile. Foster parents and siblings, cops, teachers, priests, nuns, and Eric and Mac of course. Collin couldn't answer the questions that bubbled from their bloody lips. They asked him why he let this happen, and why he didn't protect them. They asked him why he'd let himself become a monster.

Whether he couldn't take anymore, or his subconscious came to understand and accept the situation, Collin woke from his tormented slumber, to a hellish reality.

"You're awake, good, here, drink some water," said H, holding a glass out for Collin, who slowly sat up, then accepted the glass, and downed it thirstily.

"We're not evil Collin,"said Deana, "no devils or demons here."

"Ok," said Collin, sitting forward and rubbing his eyes.

"Collin," said Hamilton, "I told you of a war a while ago, and I told you that 'vampirism' can affect any species. It's only in man that Anon has seen it develop into a functioning species of it's own. And, well, it's only because of him that it has had a chance to exist. That day he let me and a few others live, he instilled in us the idea that we could live a long time, with friends and family, if we only gave up on the men in us. You see, we'd have to separate ourselves from man's incessant need to dominate. We were no longer men, and needn't be like them. Making a mark was no longer a concern, in fact, it would be better if no one knew that we existed at all. He taught us that if we contained the infection, and chose wisely who to take in, we could live a hundred lifetimes, on our terms. As Dee pointed out, no devil, no demons, it's just survival Collin. I should mention that Anon's master-plan for us also protects mankind from us."

"Can I have some more water?" asked Collin.

They were back in the war room. Deana grabbed a pitcher from the big desk and walked it over to him. She filled his glass, then returned to H's side, who was again leaning against the desk.

Collin wondered once more about the beautiful Deana. About being with her, and if there was a heart that beat within her, if she could love, or if she'd seen so many scenes like the one in the kennel that it would be a cold heart, immune to affection.

He gulped down a mouthful of water, then asked, "are you alive, dead...undead?"

"As I explained earlier," said H, "we are alive, and kept alive by a parasite that sustains itself on our blood. They cannot exist in a dead body. We are most certainly alive."

"So, your hearts are pumping, your organs still function? Why are you so cold?" asked Collin.

"Well, it's as simple as a thermostat. The parasites govern our biological and chemical functions. They need a certain climate to thrive, and they will maintain it as long as they can."

"So, they heal you, they won't let you die?" asked Collin.

"Right. The hosts death would surely be their end. I've heard of them clinging to a body for as long as a year to repair it. Once infected, it's just about impossible to incur enough damage to cause all of them to die, and the survivors will propagate and rebuild, just like man." said H.

"What about crosses? Silver and sunlight?" prodded Collin.

"Nonsense. They will die in the sun, and fire, but most other beliefs about vampires are complete fabrications. Deana here loves mirrors, don't you love?" said Hamilton.

"Don't forget about garlic," said Deana, seeming a little bored with the conversation.

"Oh, right. It's also a misconception that we don't eat food. We have to be careful though, since it's our blood that fuels them. Garlic, onions, ginger...what you might consider cleansing foods, and some acidic foods can be devastating to them. They won't die necessarily, but they will get sick, and take the host down with them." said H.

"I suppose crosses mean nothing to you...what about a stake through the heart," asked Collin.

"Crosses certainly do mean something to me, but no, they cause me no discomfort. A stake through the heart...I'd survive it, again. But, to answer your ultimate question, if you were to behead a vampire, or pluck out it's heart, it would die. I don't think that they'd survive without a heart long enough to rebuild one. But, everything has a half-life, everything dies." said H.

"What about your Anon character?" inquired Collin.

"Anon is not living matter. He's...conscious energy." answered Hamilton.

"You're making a mistake," said a husky voice.

Collin turned and looked over his shoulder to see who'd spoken, and there stood a cowboy. Duster, boots, buckle and all. Stephan's piercing blue eyes looked right through Collin who recognized the Frenchman, and the alpha werewolf immediately. He was rocking his jaw from side to side, rolling a tooth pick back and forth with his teeth.

"Are werewolves space aliens too?" asked Collin flatly.

"Who cares?" growled the cowboy.

"Stephan, he's curious," said Deana.

"Listen," said Stephan firmly, leaning against one of the

statues at the back of the room. "You just told im how to kill you and all your brodders. You fuckin' nuts? Eh? Dis guy, eez dangereux. Too strong, eez gonna turn, and eez gonna be trops puissant...uh, too powerful. You kill im now, ok, or me, uh, I will do it, Ok?"

"Collin, don't worry about him," said H with a smile, "as we respected his house, he will respect mine. Now, we know less about our friend's history than our own. Even Anon resorted to belief to cope with their up-rise. Physically, there is no difference between Stephan and yourself, scientifically speaking. Yet, he can transform at will and live four, five hundred years, but you cannot. It is believed Collin, that the legend is accurate where werewolves are concerned. It was a curse. Given life by a hatred so strong, an imagination so focused, and a belief so resilient, that it still finds the cursed thousands of years later."

"Black magic, a gypsy curse," said Collin, willing to believe just about anything at this point.

"Indeed. Absolutely. I tend to avoid 'beliefs' as much as possible...but that doesn't stop someone else from believing. What if they believe it so wholly that it's enough to make it real? I see no reason why someone who believes that they are cursed could not give life and purpose to one, a curse that is. If Anon can exist, so can anything really," stated Hamilton.

"What's going to happen to me? Can I get a straight answer on that too? Thanks," said Collin, still light-headed, but feeling stronger, and less hazy now.

"Finalement," said Stephan.

"Right, well, as I've said multiple times now, you have a choice to make." said H.

"What, I become one of you, or die, is that it?" said Collin.

"I say you die," said Stephan.

"Not so fast now big boy," said Deana flirtatiously.

"Non. I don't like im. I don't like any of it. Dere's someting about im...I don't trust im, dat's all," said Stephan.

"Yeah, well, I think that's just your ego talking. I suspect you've caught the scent of another alpha," said Deana.

"And so, so what eh? You don't tink dat ee's gonna be powerful? You are stupide. You be careful wit dis one, I fought im you know, at is boxing arene. He as, how you say, la conviction?" said Stephan.

"Conviction," stated H.

"Oui, ç'est ca...ee as conviction, and a bunch of it too eh," said Stephan's deep voice.

"Well, Collin," said Hamilton, "is there anything you'd like to say in your defence?"

Collin shook his head and took another drink of water.

"You scared boy?" asked the cowboy.

"Not anymore, not really...no," replied Collin.

"You are not scared to lose your life?" probed Stephan.

"I haven't been doin' much with it, to be honest. Only thing I keep thinking about is my truck, and how I'll never get to drive it again...and I can't even really be scared of that, because I already know it's been trashed," remarked Collin.

"Of course," smiled H, "Stephan, Collin bought a new truck today, and a trailer. He plans on building a house on wheels and travel the land...isn't that interesting?"

"Hmph," huffed Stephan.

"Stephan has a fifth-wheel," explained H, "he's been all over the Americas in it. A magnificent house like this one, and he sleeps in his trailer."

"Why would you build one when you can buy one so cheap? Stupide," asked Stephan.

"Because I know what I want," said Collin. "Always seems to be a lot of wasted space in trailers, and I never like the layouts." Collin stood and retrieved the pad of paper that lived in his jacket pocket. He walked half way to the cowboy, then stopped, and put the pad down on a tall end table that didn't seem to have a purpose other than taking up that spot. He returned to the couch and sat down.

"Check it out," said H to Stephan, who stepped casually over to the pad, picked it up and inspected some drawings while scratching at his beard.

"Oui, yes, ok, it is smart. J'aime t'es...I like your ideas, dey are good. Uh, you know, I could build dis, but uh, I would use a fif-wheel, gut it, and uh, start over." said Stephan.

"Thanks," said Collin, "but don't you want me dead?"

"Well, I tink dat you are dangereux, but I am not your mentor. You are not my problème...but, you bedder remember dat, ok. Do not piss me off mon ami," said Stephan, "I do not care about you. I eat your heart wit une salade, and some poutine, uh...and maybee, some lemon pie...comprends?"

"Am I to understand that you're changing your vote?" asked H.

"I am ere for la season, it would be a good projet. And if Collin ee pisses me off, I will keep it for me, I would like dat," said Stephan.

"But, you're not willing to mentor him," asked Deana.

"Non. Fuck dat. He is not going to be my responsabilité. No way," said Stephan.

"Fine. What say you Deana?" grinned Hamilton.

"Oh, I think it's safe to say that Collin would make a pretty addition to the family," affirmed Deana.

"And there you have it. Collin, it doesn't look like being a wolf is an option any longer. Normally, individuals in your position have been taught a great deal about us and our histories. It is usually something that they've learned to want...and have proven that want to us. They always know whether they want to be a wolf or vampire. It's my fault that this has all unravelled so chaotically, but I still know that what we have to offer is worth considering, and that you can appreciate it's significance."

"Right. And, uh, what if I'm not interested?" inquired Collin, already knowing the answer.

"Well, then, I suppose we'd have to take precautions Collin. You know who and where we are. Again, I have to apologize. Normally, a person in your position would have had time to consider their options, and been brought into a much more...agreeable environment. I wanted to get to know you, regale you with stories of wizards, mermaids and giants. Open your mind, through your imagination, then blow it...but not until I'd have known that you would in fact accept it." said H.

Collin squinted, then closed his eyes and rubbed his temples. He'd been clenching his jaw while listening to Hamilton. He had just been informed that there was a mock procedure in the process, and it made him feel angrier. He'd bypassed the monster's marketing campaign, and H was apologizing for not having followed protocol in his brainwashing. He'd gone to a job interview years earlier. It began with a seminar of sorts, and there were other candidates in attendance. It had all sounded too good to be true, but Collin was desperate for a paycheck, and believed for a while during that seminar that he was going to make a killing using the tried and proven money-making techniques these people were going to share with him. They made it sound like he and the others who'd shown up were much smarter than the rest of the population, simply for having shown up. It made Collin look around the room, and he didn't see the cream of the crop. At that moment, he realized that he was looking at suckers. That the handsome couple at the front of the room were actors, and that they were going through their lines. It turned out to be a pyramid scam, disguised as a mutual fund, and Collin was very upset with himself for getting sucked in, even if it was only for a few minutes.

He would be sitting somewhere else being fed lines instead of being here about to die if all had gone according to plan, and it angered Collin deeply. He wanted to spit in H's face, whose plan was to kill Collin's friends while he was distracted, then enslave him, while selling it all with a smile.

"So, how often do people reject your sales-pitch?" asked Collin.

"Sales-pitch? Is that how you're processing this?" asked H.

"This, no. This is entrapment. If you'd had your way, if I'd sat through all your stories, that would have been a mock sales-pitch." stated Collin.

"Wow. Does it really seem that cheap to you?" asked Hamilton.

"Whatever. As interesting as it all is, it still is what it is." said Collin, "You've known the bottom line the whole time, and I was duped. Now here I sit with an ultimatum on my hands. Didn't you promise me that my consent would be involved?"

"I did," said H.

"Yeah, well I think that you should replace my truck and let me be on my way, so I can get on with my plans...remember those?" said Collin.

"Just, let you go?" said H.

"Yep. Seriously, who the hell am I going to tell? And, if ever you decide to hunt me down, so be it, that would be much more fair than this, shit, I'm in the belly of the beast." said Collin.

"I don't think that would be much better for you Collin. Word would spread quickly...this is no belly, there are colonies everywhere, and yes, you would be hunted. As strong as you are Collin, you would lose, and you'd more than likely face a much worse fate than either of your choices here today." said H.

"Collin," said Deana, sitting on the marble desk, "you can still do everything you've ever wanted to, and then some. You'll have friends and family forever. You'll have us...me."

Collin shook his head. "So why do I feel like I just woke up on the bottom rung of a pyramid scam?"

"That's offensive, yeah, I'm offended by it." said Hamilton.

"Really? You're offended? This whole night has been an offence to me! You're trying to sell me a 'family', but I'd still just be a lackey, wouldn't I...just a different organization." suggested Collin.

"Absolutely, yes Collin. There is a hierarchy and it is to be respected. A lot of the wolves start out as cops, or infiltrate the military. Some are lawyers, judges, politicians, even scientists. We are all expected to do our part. Things are a little different for us," said Hamilton, gesturing to Deana, "as we are useless during the day, and we make people uncomfortable. But we can do wonders behind the scenes Collin, and that is where I envision you. Learning the ropes from me, working out of the parking facility of course. You would eventually replace me, and I would move up in the corporation," explained H.

"So, you're not the top guy?" asked Collin.

"No. Far from it. I was once...but that's for another time." replied H.

"Right. And, you want to recruit me to take your place...oh, and you're looking for some long-term friendship or something...people to share your hellish eternities with. Does it make it more tolerable, the endlessness of it all?" asked Collin.

"You surprise me Collin. I truly thought that you'd appreciate being accepted into a group, finding a place to fit in. I wasn't expecting you to be such a little bitch," said Hamilton. "do you have any idea how many lifetimes I've lived? Imagine the experience and knowledge base that we have. How can you, Collin McBride, stand there and lecture me. Yes Collin, a thing of key importance in any life is the connections and relations...the bonds that are formed. I thought that you would make a good friend, of that, I am guilty. But if you're accusing me of being more selfish than giving in my offer to you, then, maybe you're a little too self-centred to be a member of our community. How, after everything I've shown you tonight, can you only be thinking of yourself?"

"Are you fuckin' serious? I don't have a choice Hamilton! The only damned thing that matters is being free. Freedom to choose and do what you want with your time here. I haven't been my own man a full day, and you wonder why I'm pissed? You kill my friend, enslave another, and want me, at the flip of a switch, to just accept it all and forgive you, and look up to you?" pointed out Collin.

"Collin, I can appreciate what you're saying, absolutely, but, the thirty years or so that you've been alive is but a blink compared to what you could live. You're holding onto something that is fleeting, and in a thousand years, the fact that you didn't get to roam around in your fifth-wheel won't matter to you one bit. Hell, I can cross a continent in an evening...open your mind my friend," implored Hamilton.

"Tabar...ecoute," interrupted Stephan, "I tole you eh, dis one is too proud. I really don't tink dat you should waste your time on im. He would not even be a good worker...just kill him, find anodder one."

"I've been looking and waiting for twenty years Stephan...I thought he was the perfect candidate," said H.

"Non, dis one? I know ten guys just like im, notting special dat one," said Stephan before spitting out his toothpick.

"I beg to differ Stephan, there is more to Collin than meets the eye," said H.

"J'menfous. I am warning you Amilton, dere is too much anger in im. I bet dat he kills you if you give im your powers," urged Stephan.

"What? Nonsense," said Hamilton.

"I am telling you, I can see it in iz eyes," insisted Stephan.

"Collin," said H, "would you be so inclined to kill a 'made man' if you were a mafioso? You're not that foolish are you? Think of us in the same way. You will travel the world. You will meet many others like us, including the heads of the family, so to speak. Once one of us, you will be accountable to us. If you were to attack another member, without prior approval, there would be a bounty put out on you. Makes sense, right?"

Collin nodded. He listened while feeling like he was having deja vu. A calmness came over him as everything seemed to come together. It was as though he'd been looking at an abstract scene that was now revealing itself to him. He agreed with what Stephan was saying, and he wasn't deterred at all by the threat of a bounty on his head, he was about to die anyways.

Hamilton moved from the desk. He walked over to Stephan and put his hands on the Frenchman's shoulders, he smiled and said, "I'm late for a very important meeting."

"We are not finished ere, what about im?" said Stephan, pointing at Collin.

"Well, I'm going to have to leave him in your capable hands for now," said H.

"Is that a good idea?" asked Deana.

"I don't really have a choice," said H. "Collin, I'm sorry, but the reason that I cancelled on you today was that I was contacted by Anon, and he wanted to meet with me. I'd like to make an effort to see him if it's still possible."

"I tought ee was gone," said Stephan.

"So did I," said Hamilton.

"What do you think he wants?" asked Deana, still sitting on the desk, with her perfect legs dangling, swinging back and forth like pendulums, hypnotizing a fantasizing Collin.

"I expect that he'll want to lay some ground rules for while he's away," guessed Hamilton.

"Den, why wouldn't ee talk to da council?" inquired Stephan.

"Oh, I'm sure that he has, but he and I have a history...I like to think that we're friends, and that he wants to say goodbye, in his way," said H.

"Ok, so, you are leaving Collin for me?" asked Stephan.

"Yeah," cut in Collin, "you just planning on leaving me here?"

"Sorry Collin. Put yourself in my position. I might have just missed my last chance to see Anon," said H, walking to the door.

"I didn't ask you to do that. In fact, I didn't ask for any of this," stated Collin.

"If I hadn't shown up when I did, you'd be dead, or worse right now Collin. I chose to save your ass rather than meet with a god, because I figured that you'd be by my side for centuries to come. I must admit, I'm starting to regret my decision," said Hamilton flatly.

"Say hi to Anon for me would ya," said Collin.

Hamilton shook his head, "you just might be too stubborn, and too proud Collin...Stephan just might be right."

Collin nodded slowly in agreement, "and I don't like decisions being made for me either," he said.

"Right, well, there you have it. I'm at a loss. I was thinking that you could spend the night, I'll be back before morning, we could continue our conversation then, if you survive that long with the attitude you're giving off," said H with that smile on his lips. "Dee, sweetie, Stephan will take it from here, kindly remember your place."

Deana looked at Collin, then glared at Hamilton, then Stephan who was grinning like a little boy who'd just gotten his first peek at a woman's naked flesh.

"You messed this all to hell," she said to Hamilton.

"I know. I'm a vampire, not a god. I'll be back in a few hours, just be civil until then and we'll work it all out, fair enough?" asked Hamilton.

Collin looked to Deana who was eyeing the Frenchman who was stroking his goatee.

"Ok, until then," said H before turning and heading out of the war room.

Deana dropped her gaze to Collin who was still sitting on the couch. "Everything is going to be fine, don't worry Collin," she said.

"Yeah, everyting is going to be fine Collin...but, I tink you should worry a lot," grinned Stephan.

∞

12

Deana stood dumbfounded by Hamilton's departure, Stephan walked to the open balcony door, and Collin listened to the sound of wind chimes as he watched the Frenchman step outside. Then he looked to Deana who was once again looking very sad.

He stood up and walked over to her, and she gracefully moved from the desk to meet him. They stood close to each other, staring into each others faces, each trying to memorize every detail.

"So," said Collin, "what are my chances?"

"Not very good," said Deana, looking out at Stephan.

"You're...you're so fuckin' beautiful Deana. If I die, I hope there isn't an after-life...cause I don't want to remember being torn from you...I'd be pissed for all eternity," confessed Collin.

Deana smiled sweetly and moved closer to him. They stood inches apart. She could feel the heat coming off of his body, and he barely noticed the musty odor as she leaned into him, resting a cheek on his chest. Her breasts pressed against him as she wrapped her arms around him and squeezed him tight. She felt so good, and Collin took her in his arms, embracing her with all the tenderness that he could muster while so much anger boiled within him. He'd only just met her, but Collin was in more than a little danger of falling wholly and completely for her. He felt that he was somehow supposed to meet her. He was never so sure of who he was and what he wanted than when he was with her. Deana made him feel like he'd lived his entire life without the most essential element...her. He whispered into her ear, "what if I told you that I was going to survive this?"

"I'd say that's wonderful...and that, he can still hear you," replied Deana.

"I know it sounds silly," he whispered, "but I just have this feeling that it's not over for me, not for a long shot...it's all going to be ok."

"Like the wildebeest and the crocodile..." she said into his chest. Then she looked up into his eyes. Their noses touched and on their lips they felt each others breath. They felt the beating of their hearts merge. It relaxed Collin, and angered him even more.

"Can I ask you something?" whispered Collin. "Do you...do vampires, make love?"

Deana smiled her sweet, seductive and mischievous smile while nodding and looking up at him with her mystical eyes.

"And, uh...do I get a last wish?" asked Collin with a sheepish grin.

"Oh...you're bad Collin," said Deana, glancing out to the cowboy on the balcony. "Listen, he has a bit of a thing for me...you're going to infuriate him."

"If anyone has the right to be furious here tonight, it's me," said Collin, "I don't care if he's jealous, in fact, I like the idea of getting under his skin. Hamilton told me that the beast doesn't care about anything...doesn't want anything...guess he does have a weakness."

"Hamilton doesn't see everything, and he ignores anything that doesn't have to do with him," said Deana.

"Yeah, are all vamps as selfish as him?" asked Collin.

"Vamps," said Deana, "nice...no Collin, but for the most part, yes, no question about it. You have to like yourself quite a bit to be immortal. That, or have a deep enough hatred to carry you, one or the other, for the most part."

"What about you? What drives you?" asked Collin, his hands on the small of her back, pulling her hips into his.

"I'm easily entertained," answered Deana.

"Den she get bored easy too eh," added the cowboy from the balcony, looking out at the still water.

"Mind your business," snapped Deana.

Stephen moved from the balcony railing to the doorway. "You," he said, pointing at Collin, "I don't trust you...but her," he said, now pointing at Deana, "I trust her even less callisse."

"Thanks, good to know," said Collin dryly.

"Ok, you know what, dat's enough of dis shit. Come on, get da fuck out ere, let's finish dis," said Stephan firmly.

"Whoa, whoa tabarnac," said Deana, "finish what? What are you rushing at Stephan?"

"You know what, don't play stupide," blurted Stephan.

"No, I don't know what. I didn't hear anything concrete. Hamilton said he'd be back by morning, nothing was decided beyond that," pointed out Deana.

"Den, you are fooling yourself. You eard it just like me. I'm in charge eh, I decide. And uh, Hamilton, ee knows what I decide," said Stephan.

"I won't let you hurt him Steph, why don't you go check on your rat pack," spat Deana.

"Ma p'tite salope...Fuck you...you get in my way, you disobey me, and I'll hurt you real bad, ok? Give me a raison, please," invited Stephan.

"Alright, no reason to threaten the lady," said Collin as he let go of Deana and stepped in between her and the Frenchman, who was laughing a deep, slow, muwahaha laugh, like some evil cartoon genius.

"I like to see you try and stop me," challenged Stephan.

Deana moved to Collin's side, "thank you Collin, but I don't need your protection, I'm not scared of him." She took his hand into hers, "I'll take care of you, how's that sound?"

"Salope! You fuckin' slut, go away! Dis is business," barked

Stephan.

"You can call me whatever you want, but who's the jealous bitch around here?" said Deana with a smirk.

"Jealous? You tink I'm jealous of a dead man?" said the cowboy.

"I'm not dead yet Toto," smiled Collin.

"Collin, please...I'll handle this," said Deana sternly.

Collin took a few steps towards the balcony and Stephan. "If you're planning on taking me out, you better make sure you do it right. Leave an inch of life in me, and I swear to you Alpo breath, I will have my vengeance."

"That's really not helping," said Deana, as Stephan grinned widely and tipped his hat.

"No weapons, no fangs...you man enough to put me down frenchy?" chirped Collin.

The cowboy's hands clenched into fists. He bent at the knees and swayed from foot to foot. "I don't need fangs for you pecker-ead...you hit like a little girl."

"Don't be a fool," urged Deana as Collin moved again towards the balcony.

"It was a pleasure meeting you Deana," said Collin, continuing on towards Stephan, who was repeatedly opening and clenching his fists while bobbing up and down, and side to side.

"Make it count frog," taunted Collin, getting the desired reaction.

The cowboy lunged, he was all attack, no defence, both hands reaching for Collin's shoulders and looking like he was going to bite at Collin's face if given the chance. Collin was still advancing on the Frenchman, and was able to step into a powerful knee thrust that winded Stephan, who's feet came off the ground with the force of the blow. His arms dropped immediately to guard his body as he gasped loudly for air. Collin saw surprise and shock in his opponents eyes, and drove his left hand in an uppercut to his chin, knocking the wolfman reeling back. Collin then slammed a straight right into an unprotected throat, and Stephan dropped like a shot, convulsing and flopping around, futilely trying to push himself away from Collin with his feet, his boot heels just scuffing off the smooth floor.

Collin's hand went to the but of his gun, it was instinct, and he heard Deana confirm what had just run through his mind. "If you shoot him, everyone's going to come running."

Collin McBride then hunkered down, kneeling on Stephan's chest while he continued to clutch at his throat and gasp in a panic. He pulled his dagger from it's sheath. He held it out in front of the Frenchman's face. "Beauty, isn't it?" Stephan's eyes moved from the blood-streaked blade to the blood stained Collin. "Guess we had a deal...no weapons...you do realize I can kill you without one right now, don't you? Couple more neck shots, shit, I could tare out your throat. How's about a new deal? I let you live, and you leave me the fuck alone. Sound good to you?"

Stephan's body heaved as he tried to roll out from under Collin, but he was being held firmly in place by knees pushing down on his shoulders. Collin reached under the cowboy's head, grabbing a fistful of hair. He gave it a tug, "whattaya say? Wanna make a deal?" Nothing but the sound of clicks, choking and gasping answered his question. "Just nod or shake your head...do you want to live?"

Stephan still didn't react to the question. He simply stared up at Collin with rage and hatred in his eyes.

"Can I make a suggestion?" asked Deana, "let's just go. I'll take you to a car, you can escape. If you kill him, you'll be hunted everywhere you go. Collin, come on, you can take the Camaro, sell it, I don't care...take advantage of the few minutes you have...let's go!"

Collin looked up to Deana who was standing, looking anxious with her hands cupped to her bosom like she was praying. "I walk away, and he'll hunt me down, no?"

"Kill him, and it'll be his entire pack that hunts you, and then some. You'll be a wanted man Collin, and you won't be safe anywhere," she said sadly.

Stephan's eyes followed the conversation while he continued to protect his neck, trying to draw a lungful of air, and Deana knew full-well that one breath would be all it would take to overturn Collin's victory.

"Collin, it's lose-lose. Come on, I'll take you to the car and make sure you get out of here," affirmed Deana.

"Ok," said Collin as he rose from the still-reeling cowboy,

"alright, get me outta this madhouse."

"We have to get to the other end of the house, to the garage," said Deana.

Collin looked down at Stephan and said, "see ya around," then he turned and headed for Deana, and the door, but the cowboy grabbed each of his ankles with a steely grip.

Collin looked back down in time to see the Frenchman sucking in some air through his teeth. "Oh shit," said Collin under his breath. He tried to kick his feet free, but Stephan's hold didn't lax, to the contrary, it tightened, intensely.

The beautiful bald brick-house watched in horror as Stephan drew another breath, smiled menacingly, and began to laugh his muwaha laugh. He gasped again between chuckles, a deep breath, then continued laughing, getting deeper and raspier with each outburst.

Claws punctured Collin's ankles, he groaned, the pain was excruciating. They sank deeper as the claws grew longer, wider and thicker, piercing muscle, tendons and ligaments.

"Stop Stephan!" yelled Deana, but to no avail, he was transforming into the beast.

The first thing that Collin noticed was the hair that slithered out from every pore on the cowboy's face. Within seconds, he was covered in long black and silver fur. The Frenchman's brow, cheeks and nose jutted out to the sound of crunching bone and cartilage, and of course, the deep crackling laugh that was now starting to sound more like coughs and pants.

Buttons from Stephan's shirt popped one by one, flung through the air from the force of his swelling body. It was like watching a bag full of gremlins as they writhed and pushed to get out. Collin stared, frozen mentally and shackled physically by powerful hands with razor-like claws. He watched and heard the man's jaw become the beast's, exploding with muscle at the jawline and pushing forward at the mouth, pulling the nose out with it. The teeth stretched and swelled into long sharp fangs. The eyes changed from blue to green and doubled in size, and they looked pissed.

Collin was trying to take it all in, the sheen in the beasts eyes, it's black gums and tongue, when in a moment of terror, the wolfman spread Collin's feet apart. He was flexible, but no gymnast, and he lost his balance while the beast forced him into an involuntary split. He fell forward and readied his blade to take his weight. It was gripped in his left hand, with the blade poised to sink into the animal's neck.

He felt his ankles being shredded by the claws that didn't let up. He was going to plunge the blade into the wolf's neck and yank it out the other side as hard as he could, when, with only inches between the knife's tip and it's target, there was a flash of teeth and fur. It happened so fast that Collin barely saw it, but he felt it. The werewolf was latched onto his forearm, chomping and shaking it around like a chew toy.

The beast had bitten clean through Collin's leather sleeve, and he could feel his warm slick blood running down his wrist. He released his knife, it fell beside the monster's head. Collin picked it up with his free hand and quickly slashed once across the wolf's nose, then sank it into it's neck.

The next thing he knew, Collin was spiralling through the air. He hit the top of the door frame with his chest and face. His legs kept going, and they pulled him out onto the balcony, twisting in flight, trying to control his fall. Unfortunately, he didn't get to pilot his descent to the stone floor that awaited patiently. He was able to get his injured forearm between his face and the ground, but the force of landing dislocated his shoulder and darn near broke his neck. His lower back, hips and legs hit the stone just as hard with a smack, and Collin cried out in agony.

He couldn't remember ever having felt that kind of shock. Every square inch of him was screaming and burning with pain. He could taste blood, and was sure that his nose was broken, maybe even his jaw. He didn't want to move a muscle, but quickly realized that he was still under attack. He rolled over and with great effort got to one knee. The monster was in the same position, watching him, grinning.

Collin saw his knife, it was only feet from him in the doorway. He looked at the werewolf and it hunkered down, preparing itself to leap. Collin pushed off, lunging for his weapon, but his ankle gave out on him, he fell inches short, and he had to scramble to get a hold of it. He kept an eye on the beast, and saw it closing the gap at an alarming speed. He rolled to his left, coming out of it squatting on the balls of his feet, and he realized two things balancing himself that way. The first was that his ankles were about to buckle, and the other, that he was about to be rammed by a snarling mass of muscle and fur, and he wasn't ready for it.

He started to fall backwards and quickly gave up on trying to brace himself. He focused all of his energy on the blade in his right hand and the moment to strike. He cocked his arm in order to be able to greet the beast properly, but it was on top of him sooner than he could strike.

The monster didn't claw at Collin or try to hit him, no, the beast collided with Collin's shoulder fangs first, driving them into his collar bone and shoulder blade. The momentum of the attack knocked Collin off his feet. He was driven back by the tackle into the stone railing, forcing the wind from his lungs.

The silver-streaked werewolf withdrew it's long fangs from Collin's meaty shoulder after giving his entire body a shake, but the lack of teeth in him was a short-lived relief. Ten jagged claws sank ever so slowly into his abdomen as the wolf leaned into Collin, pushing it's nose and forehead against Collin's, glaring into his eyes, which were only inches from each other.

Collin drove his right fist into the wolf's temple twice, then once to a kidney, but the beast kept pressing those nasty claws deeper into his stomach and sides, inch by inch, and the monster was definitely taking pleasure in it.

Collin was being bent backwards by the creature that towered over him, and it continued to push Collin's head back with it's own face. It's slobber slicking Collin's cheeks and neck. He felt like he was going to break in two. Stephan was standing on his feet, pinning them to the floor, and he was going to snap Collin's back if nothing was done about it. Nothing was, and after a long moment of intense pain, where the stretching became ripping, there was a loud pop, and it was done.

The wolf chuckled, sounding more like it was choking, and Collin felt it's cheeks rise on his own as the monster grinned and drooled on his chin and into his mouth. He bashed his fist against the Manimal's head, ribs and side as hard as he could, for as long as he could, but he was still trying to get a decent lungful of air and wrap his mind around the fact that his legs were now useless.

The wolf didn't seem to feel the blows, even a little, and it kept pressing into Collin, until finally, the beast pulled it's head back. It opened it's mouth wide, it's eyes flashed, then it slammed it's face into Collin's chest, who was still doubled over the balcony railing. Stephan bit out chunk after chunk of flesh from the muscular chest, digging it would seem, for the heart that pounded beneath it.

Collin cried out again, in pain and terror. He wasn't so sure that he'd survive to avenge himself and his friends, who he'd been unable to protect. He could only avenge, or die, and the decision was being made for him.

The wolf was about to chomp down again when it's body tensed and it yelped in Collin's face with bewilderment in it's eyes. He couldn't see it, but Deana had chosen a side, his, and she'd just sank Tesan Uvol's dagger into the mandog's neck and was repeatedly driving it home to the hilt.

Stephan yanked his fingers out of Collin's torso, then spun, striking Deana across the face with his forearm, sending her sprawling into the wall. Collin saw some of it while his body slid over the railing. He was weak, in shock, and he was a mess with blood. It all made his attempt to grab onto the railing impossible.

He fell a good fifteen feet into a rosebush, flat on his face and stomach. Out of breath again, he struggled to look up, and saw the werewolf looking down at him. It hopped up onto the railing, clacked it jaws together a few times, then jump up high, targeting Collin as a cushioning for it's landing.

In mid-air, the monster jerked it's head in surprise in time to see a blur, which Collin saw too. It smashed into the beast and they disappeared like a rocket into the darkness. A fight ensued, Collin could hear it, but had no clue who was winning. He was dying in a rosebush, listening to the battle, thinking to himself that he had to get to the water. He used his one good appendage and tried to pull himself out of the rosebush, towards the lake. A few inches at a time was all he could manage, but he kept going, digging his fingers into grass and dirt, pulling with everything he had, fuelled by the need to survive, so that he could avenge himself, and, finally have love in his life.

He heard a grunt, then a roar, a wet smack and bones breaking. There was a thud and a woman's cry, then a yelp, choking, then silence. Collin couldn't be sure of what had just gone down or who the victor had been. He stopped his efforts, listening, laying face down in the dirt, covered in blood from head to toe. He didn't hear anything coming from where Stephan and Deana had vanished. He tried again to pull himself to the water, grabbing a handful of lawn and pulling hard. The grass gave way in his hand, so he pushed his fingers into the ground and tried again. Over and over he pulled himself along the ground a few inches at a time. He'd stop to listen, then continue the process, gaining a few feet over the course of a minute.

His hopes were returning when a wave of lightness washed

over him. He felt cold and his eyes grew heavy, his ears felt hot, and all he could think about was how great some sleep would be.

In the next moment, he was dreaming. He was in a boardroom, at the head of the table. He was sitting with a room-full of people that he mostly didn't recognize, but he sensed that they all feared him.

Hamilton, Stephan and Deana were there, and they, like all the others, were dead. They were frowning, nodding, talking with their hands, but they were dead. Mauled and torn to shreds, but sitting here with him discussing the devastation that he, Collin, had wrought on mankind, on vampires, werewolves, and how he'd brought the fight to a god on another world. They all laughed, and laughed hard at how petty, selfish and futile Collin was. They laughed at his anger, he got mad and they laughed harder.

The dream was interrupted when he became aware that someone had just pulled him out of his jacket, and picked him up like a fallen child. He felt as though he was in a dream that he couldn't wake from. Even the fear that the monster was about to finish him off was distant from wherever he was now. He was disconnected from his senses, from his body, and he accepted that he was about to die, even though it pissed him off terribly.

"I've got you...you'll be fine...I'm sorry Collin." He heard the voice, and felt it's breath on his neck and ear. It was Deana, she was whispering to him, and carrying him to safety.

He felt her hand on his face. He tried to open his eyes, and got a glimpse of her beautiful smiling face, and her hair which was blowing in the wind. Then he felt the strong breeze, and he could hear clothing flapping. He rolled his head and opened his eyes again. What he saw didn't register, so he took another peek. He thought that he saw a shimmer, like light on water. Then he heard the whispering, "it's the only way...I'm so sorry baby." Deana was then cradling his head. He felt her lips on his, then they moved across his cheek and down to his neck. He felt her tongue on his skin, then a pinch. He opened his eyes with a gasp and saw stars before everything faded again.

He was dreaming once more. This time, he was making love with Deana. She was kissing him tenderly, running her fingers across the back of his head. He could taste her, and he sucked on her sweet lips, until the taste changed. It became bitter and metallic, and he choked.

Collin came to with Deana's wrist in his mouth. He was choking on the blood that he'd been lapping up. She pulled her arm away and kissed him gently.

"They'll find you within hours anywhere on land. I don't know what else to do...you need to heal, if you survive." said Deana.

Collin tried to ask her what was happening, but he was dry, weak, and words were impossible.

"You know where I'll be Collin...come back to me," said Deana as she dropped Collin into the water a few kilometers off shore.

Collin felt himself falling and heard the air rushing by, but he only had a moment to realize it before he hit the water. All he could do, sinking to the depths of Lake Huron was hold his breath until another dream enfolded him. A dream of blood and gore. A dream of passion and enlightenment. A dream of hellish retribution that ended with the downfall of a god and all that it cherished.

∞

Author's two cents

Well, that was a bummer, eh boys and girls? It certainly looks like Collin's got some time to think about things, worry about Deana while laying at the bottom of a pretty big lake in a soggy weed-bed with a broken back. Werewolf and vampire bites to top off the busted face, arm, and shredded chest.

Now, you might be asking yourself how one rough Friday for one dude could endanger the entire planet, but it did. If you think that's a lot of vengeance for one person, you're right. What Collin didn't reveal about himself, in fact, he'd fooled himself about it, was that his anger had never really subsided. His intolerance had grown in him like a fungus, until he was at ease with the knot of twisted fury that was suppressed in his gut.

Whether you think that he's a good guy or not is a matter of perspective. What I want this afterword to reflect is that, it wasn't a lone freaky Friday that fuelled the chaos that lies ahead. What happened that night was the catalyst, but it isn't what carried the rage for as long as it did. It was his disgust with society as a whole, and maybe, if he was able to see it, how what he thought of it, was a critique of himself. How long, and how far can the hate for oneself carry a story? How many people can be destroyed by one man's bloody tale? When the things that live in the corner of your eye step out from the darkness, ask them, they can show you. Or, you can wait for me to tell you myself, which would be my great pleasure. Till then, enjoy.

About the Author

Paul resides in Ontario, Canada, near Lake Huron. He shares his house with his demon-dog, Beth, who was professionally trained to keep Mr. Labonte's hallucinatory visitors at bay. She's also very adept at finding and retrieving his aluminium foil hats. She's a good dog...poor thing.

He's the kind of jerk that distracts you at the grocery store, by pointing at something obscure down one of the isles, then sprays your crotch with Windex while you're otherwise occupied.

Since I'm writing this about myself, I recommend that you not believe too much of it, or any of it for that matter. I wouldn't even believe that you're not supposed to believe me, just sayin', fair enough?

Ok, the author will try to engage and challenge you, because he likes doing it. He will sometimes attempt to have you question the things that you take for granted, while he plays the devil's advocate, and looks for alternative points of views to be considered. He's very confused, which kind of helps, actually.

Paul has not written any other titles, in full...but has three side stories on the go as he works his way through book 2 of this series.

You can learn and see more if you visit him on his facebook author page. Paul J. Labonte with stories from the corner of your eye.